DRIP DROP DEAD

BOOKS BY WILLOW ROSE

Emma Frost Mysteries

Itsy Bitsy Spider

Miss Polly Had a Dolly

Run, Run, as Fast as You Can

Cross Your Heart and Hope to Die

Peek a Boo, I See You

Tweedledum and Tweedledee

Easy as One, Two, Three

There's No Place Like Home

Needles and Pins

Where the Wild Roses Grow

Waltzing Matilda

Black Frost

Detective Billie Ann Wilde series

Don't Let Her Go

Then She's Gone

In Her Grave

DRIP DROP DEAD

WILLOW ROSE

bookouture

Published by Bookouture in 2024

An imprint of Storyfire Ltd.
Carmelite House
50 Victoria Embankment
London EC4Y 0DZ

www.bookouture.com

First published by Buoy Media LLC in 2018.

ISBN: 978-1-83525-343-4
eBook ISBN: 978-1-83525-342-7

CONTENT NOTE

This book features graphic scenes of violence. If this is potentially sensitive to you, please read with care.

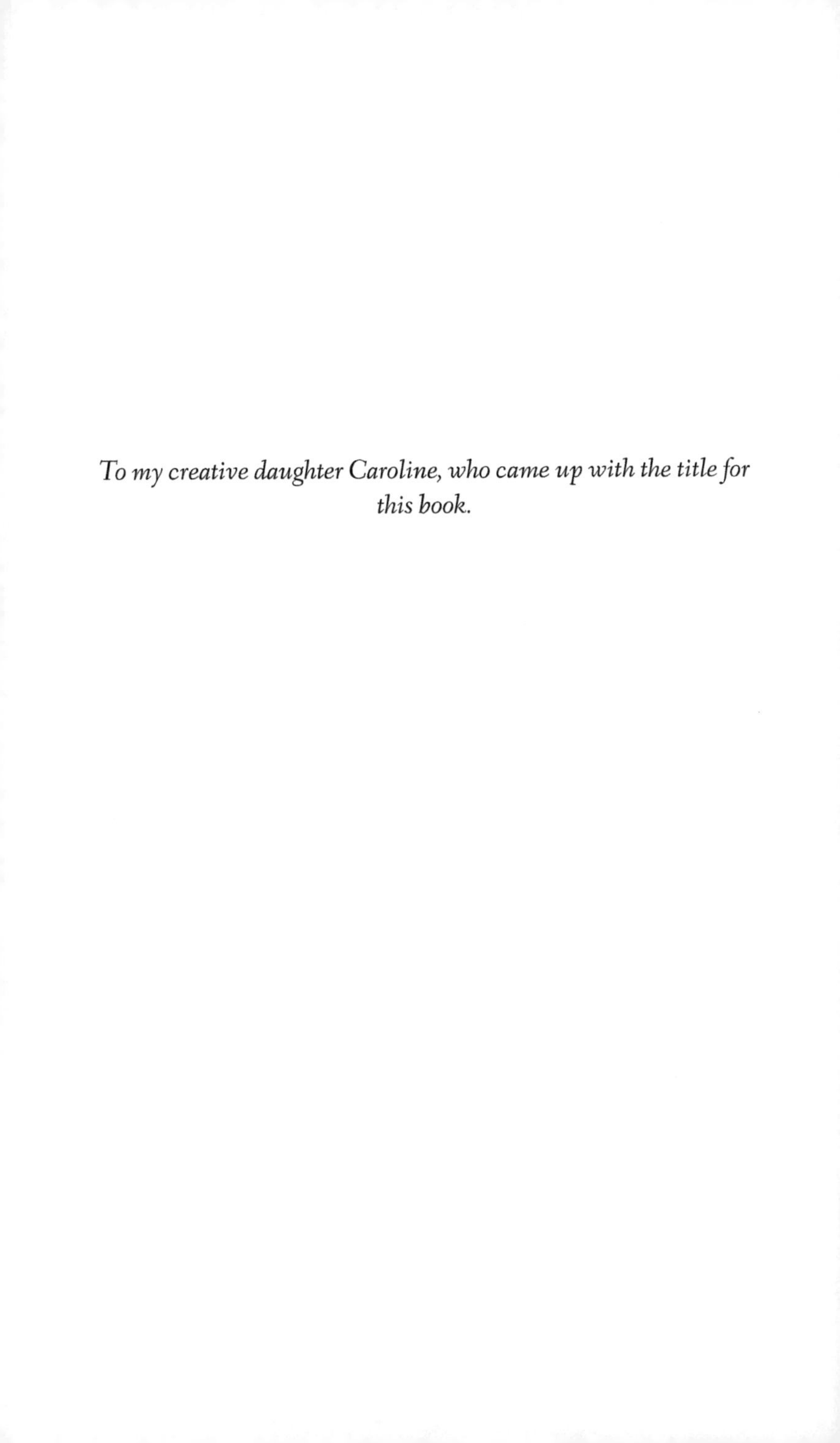

To my creative daughter Caroline, who came up with the title for this book.

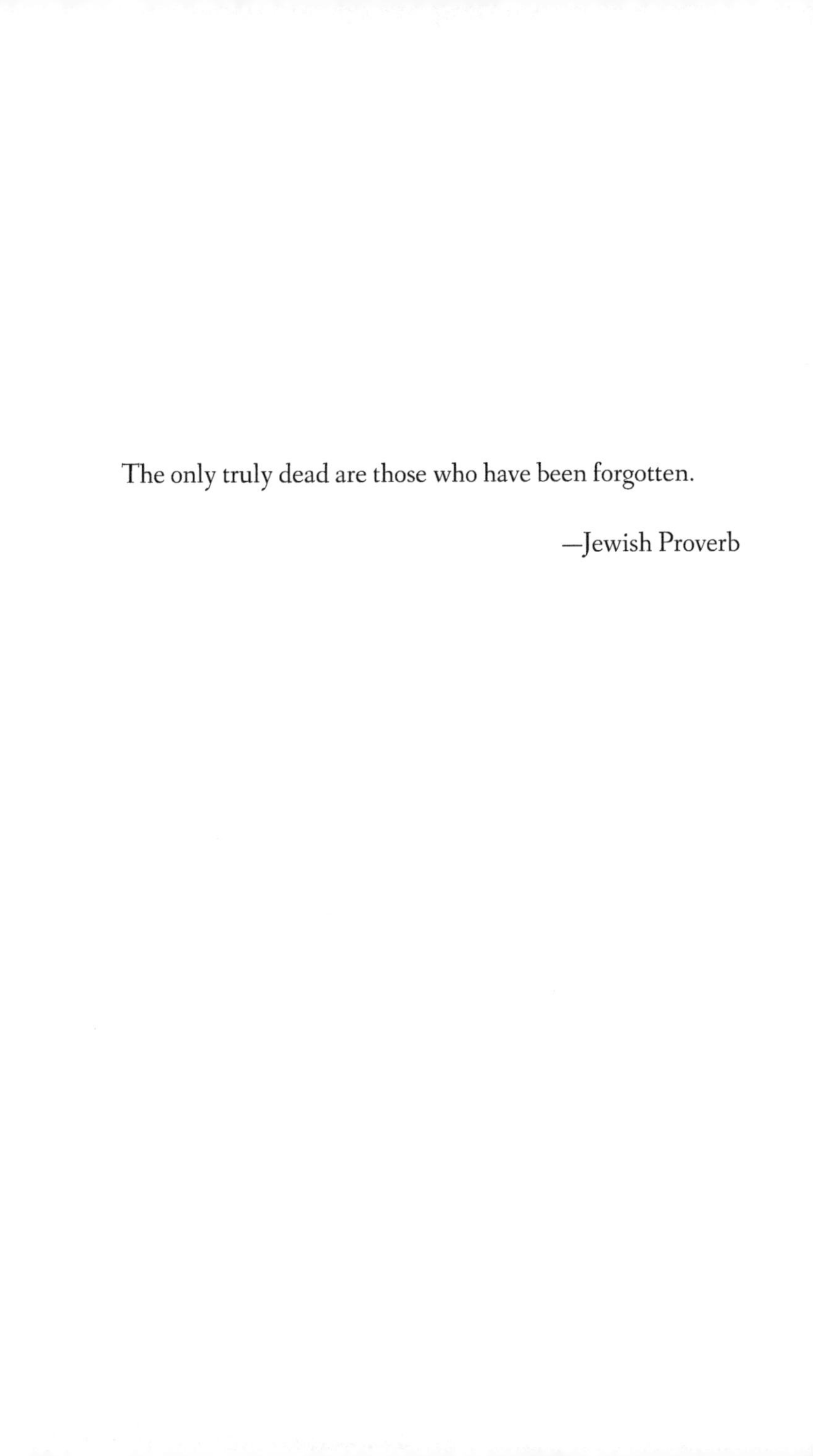

The only truly dead are those who have been forgotten.

—Jewish Proverb

ONE

It was a day like most others to Ann Mortensen. She woke up after an uneasy night's sleep, dreaming about the girl—if you could call her that—once again. She had her coffee in the kitchen and her breakfast, toasted bread and soft-boiled egg, as usual, while reading the paper, the *Fanoe Gazette*.

After her coffee, she liked to take a stroll around the lake, feeding the ducks and watching the kids skate. The bigger boys were playing hockey with old, taped sticks while the younger kids were goofing around. The ice was safe to walk on, the sign on the side said, but every now and then, it creaked and groaned mysteriously underneath them.

She watched the kids on the ice, then felt the need to use a restroom. She walked to a public restroom by the lake and went inside. And that was when she felt it. The sensation that someone was watching her. She had felt it before but never as strong as it was at this instant. It left her feeling nervous and, instead of using the restroom, she left to go home and grab one of her pills.

Her husband, Brian, didn't know about her anxiety attacks and bouts of paranoia, and she hid the pills from him. She could hardly tell him she was sensing and hearing things that weren't really there. He would only worry, and she didn't want that.

The attacks had begun after she was fired five months back... or forced into early retirement as her employer had so diplomatically put it. Her doctor believed the attacks might have to do with the fact that Ann didn't work anymore and had told her to find a hobby. Something to keep her busy and keep her mind off those thoughts that constantly lingered in the back of her mind.

What I did was wrong.

Ann sighed and put the pills back in the cabinet, hiding them behind an old box of tampons that she kept in the house for her daughter when she visited from Copenhagen. At the age of fifty-nine, Ann no longer had any use for them, but they served well as a way to cover the pills because Brian would never touch them or think to look behind them.

Ann looked at her own reflection. She had gotten old, and she even felt old. It was tough seeing Brian go off to work every day while all she did was hang around and wait for... for what? To grow old? To die?

She had loved her work, at least she used to. She loved feeling important, feeling like she made a difference in the world. But now... now, all she was left with was this old, wrinkled face looking back at her.

It will haunt me until the end of my days.

Ann thought she heard something, like the sound of something slithering. Not a snake, but similar. Bigger than a snake. And wet. Something wet. A dripping sound followed. She was certain it was coming from the shower behind her and turned to look. There was nothing there, as usual. Still, she felt like she was being observed, like someone was looking at her, watching her every move.

"I've got to stop doing this to myself."

She turned and looked at her reflection once again, saying

the words. The dripping returned, but now she refused to turn her head and look. She had heard that slithering sound when walking past the storm drain in the street outside. It sounded like when Brian was slurping his coffee, which Ann loathed.

She closed her eyes and thought of something else, of the beach, of summer, and of her grandkids playing in the waves. Ann was so much looking forward to them coming this July.

Ann opened her eyes again and was met by her own reflection, then she shivered. She grabbed her hair and felt it. She really should see a hairdresser soon. She was letting herself go.

How about today?

"Why not?" she asked herself. "I can do anything I want today. And tomorrow and the day after that. Anything I'd like. Anything."

Because nobody needs me anymore.

TWO

"Maybe we should give you some highlights. To lift it a little. Or maybe a full color."

It was a new hairdresser who took care of her at the salon. Her name was Hannah, she told her. Her hair was purple on one side and steel gray on the other. It was boyishly short and seemed unruly, but that was probably the intention, Ann concluded. The messy look was in right now, it said in all the magazines.

"Sure. I'm ready to try something new. Why not?"

"Okay, let's do it. You're gonna absolutely love it," Hannah said and, as she said it, Ann immediately regretted her decision. This girl was fresh out of school and wanted to try everything she had learned.

I'm going to end up looking like her, aren't I?

"So... gray is the new color, like steel gray," she said and showed Ann a magazine with these gorgeous gray-haired women who couldn't be more than twenty. It didn't look anything like Ann's gray hair. Hers was stiff and impossible to control. Theirs was wavy and smooth and looked gorgeous.

"Do you want that?"

"I already have gray hair," Ann said. "Why would I want to color it gray? I want you to cover the gray."

Hannah looked surprised and slightly disappointed. "Oh."

She turned a few pages in the magazine, then said, "It's just that e-e-everyone is doing the gray now."

"That might be, but I am not," Ann said. "Just give me a nice brown color. Maybe some highlights."

Hannah forced a smile and closed the magazine. "Okay."

Ann submerged herself in the stack of tabloid magazines and caught up on all the gossip there was to know about the royal family and all the TV stars in the country, the stuff that people simply had to know if they were going to be able to join in on the conversation at dinner parties. And Ann really wanted to. She had started seeing some of her old friends for brunch once a week at Café Mimosa downtown, but she never knew what to talk to them about because their worlds were so different.

As Hannah washed out the color from Ann's hair, she heard it again. At first, she thought it was the hose or the tap that made those slithering, slurping sounds. It was a wet crackle like something slimy was moving slowly inside the drain.

Ann gasped and lifted her head from the sink.

"Whoa," Hannah said. "I'm not quite done."

Ann looked at the sink, at the drain beneath her head, but there was nothing there. She closed her eyes and tried to think of something else, something that made her happy.

My grandchildren running in the sand. Alberte with a bucket in her hand, giggling.

"Is everything all right, ma'am?" Hannah asked.

Ann opened her eyes again, then nodded. "I'm sorry. I just get a little... sometimes."

"You're not feeling okay?"

Ann breathed in a few times, deep breaths like that article

had told her, the one called "Panic Attacks and How to Avoid Them Ruining Your Day." She shook her head.

"I'm fine. I'm just fine. It's just that... noise." She wrinkled her nose, then looked at the drain once again.

Hannah stared at her.

"It's just the water," she said.

"I know. I know. I just can't stand it."

Ann put her head back in the sink and closed her eyes while Hannah gently washed out the last remnants of the color. Ann worked hard on her breathing exercises, trying to keep out the overwhelming noise coming from the drain below.

THREE

She rushed out of the salon and into the street where she had parked her car, barely hearing the slushing sound as it moved in the storm drain beneath the pavement.

She started the car, then turned the music up loud and drove off. Finally, she couldn't hear it anymore. If the sound was still in her head, the music managed to drown it out.

She had heard the sound for quite some time now... for at least a week. It was everywhere she went. Except in places with loud noises or music. But it was surprisingly quiet on Fanoe island in most places. It was especially bad at night. She would lie awake and listen to it for hours without being able to figure out where it came from.

Some nights, she had even gotten out of bed to search for its origin, and she always ended up by the sink in the bathroom or the toilet, and sometimes she wondered what on earth could be in there, in her drain, but then she would hear the sound in other places in town as well and, little by little, she realized it had to be all in her head.

Ann parked the car outside the house, then turned the music off, cautiously. She sat for a few seconds and listened, but there was nothing. Ann breathed a sigh of relief. She looked at herself in the mirror and felt pretty good about her hair. Now, all she needed was to put on a little makeup, and she wouldn't look half bad. Brian was going to get a little surprise when he returned from work.

Ann rushed inside and pulled out the roast she had decided to make for tonight. She wasn't much of a housewife, but since she now had more time available in her day, she had decided to try a little harder to be the wife Brian had always wanted her to be.

"You are so much more than your career," he had said when she had told him about her early retirement, crying. "I always believed you were. You've given everything. Now, it's time for you to do something for yourself for a change."

Ann wasn't so sure she was very good at all this doing-something-for-yourself stuff. So far, it had only plunged her into an instability that she had no idea how to place or what to do with. The pills didn't always work, and she was beginning to wonder if she should start seeing a therapist. She just felt like such a failure.

Ann walked to the bathroom to pee and sat down. Lately, she hadn't been very fond of going because in bathroom the sound was worse than anywhere else. Maybe it was the quietness because she was all alone with her thoughts. Maybe it was something else.

Ann held her breath as she went, then hurried to wash her hands and rushed out of the bathroom once again, closing the door firmly behind her.

She went to the kitchen and finished prepping the roast and prepared the potatoes. A few hours later, she had dressed in a nice red dress and was sitting at the kitchen table, waiting for Brian to come home so she could surprise him with her new hair and a nice home-cooked meal.

But as the hours passed and he didn't come, Ann ended up

eating alone like so many times before. Brian had probably been hung up at work, she thought, and looked at her phone every five minutes to check if it was still working.

When the clock in the hallway struck eleven, Ann decided to go to bed. It wasn't unusual for Brian to work overtime, and usually, she would just turn in, but tonight she was sad in doing so.

"He didn't even get to see my new hair," she said to her reflection. "Tomorrow, when I wake up, it's going to be all messed up."

She brushed her teeth and removed her makeup and washed her face till the same old woman from this morning was back. Ann sighed and pulled her cheeks backward to smooth out the wrinkles and see what she would look like if she had a facelift. When she let go of it, it seemed even worse than before.

It was no use.

Ann turned off the lights in the bathroom, then closed the door to block out the slithering sound and hopefully get a good night's sleep. She crept under the covers and closed her eyes. In the distance, she could hear something, a mass of some sort slithering and sizzling up through the drain, then landing on the tile in the bathroom, but Ann was certain it was all in her mind.

It wasn't until it slid underneath the door and toward her bed, then stood above her, dripping onto the carpet, forcing water inside her mouth and down her throat, shoving the liquid into her lungs, that she finally realized that she had been right all this time.

FOUR

"We can't publish this."

The words fell, and I heard them, but I didn't believe them. They came from my publisher, Inger. We were sitting in her office at my publishing house in Copenhagen. It had taken me three hours to get there and for what? To hear her tell me she wasn't going to publish my book. I was stunned. I thought I was going there to sign the contract as I usually did at this point in the process.

"What?" I asked. "Why?"

Inger sighed. "It's too weird."

"It's too weird?"

"Emma, for God's sake. It's a book about a vampire from another world, maybe from outer space, who kidnaps and drains young people of their blood because it is special and can keep him alive for decades."

"Yes, the blood was injected into them when they were abducted, and he needed it to survive. Why can't you publish it? You always publish everything I write, and we sell millions of books."

"I don't even have a category to put it in. What genre is this?

Who am I going to sell this book to? Who is going to believe it?" she asked, holding up the manuscript with the title *Waltzing Matilda* printed on the first page.

"Does it matter?" I asked. "Isn't it enough that it's a good story?"

"But, Emma, your books are always based on real events; that's what makes them so amazing," Inger said.

"But this *is* based on real events. It happened," I said. "Last month. That's why I wrote the book."

Inger sighed and leaned back in her leather chair. Behind her was the view of Copenhagen. I liked being back for a visit, but I couldn't say I had missed the place. My heart belonged to Fanoe island now.

"I don't know what you think happened, but this book isn't real, Emma. A vampire who has been here for centuries entering through... the sewers."

"Well, we don't know how he entered, just that he woke up in the sewers under Fanoe island and, ever since, he has lived there, feeding off whomever he could hold captive until he could find other people from his own world who had also ended up there. He could recognize them by their blood, and drinking theirs would keep him—"

"Emma, I'm going to stop you right there. I've read the book. You don't have to explain it to me. I'm doing you a favor. By not publishing the book, I am saving you from public embarrassment; believe me."

"Why?" I asked. "Because it's supernatural? Because it's out of your comfort zone?"

"Because it's too darn crazy. This book will make people lose their confidence in you; you'll lose the credibility that you've built up over the years. Now, they'll start believing you are making all of it up and in that way all your other books will lose their special touch. Can't you see that?"

I shrugged. "Isn't that my problem? If I want to publish this book and ruin my credibility. This is an important story to tell. People should know about these things."

"About strange creatures living among us drinking our blood. About kids with special skills who can explode windows and create fire with their hands. I hardly think that is important to tell people, Emma. They won't believe a word of it."

"But..."

Inger shook her head. She pushed the manuscript across her desk toward me. "It's a no, Emma. I have strict orders from above. There is no way this company is publishing that book. I am sorry... no. You know what? I'm not sorry. I'm helping you out here. You should thank me."

I grabbed the manuscript between my hands and rose to my feet, holding it tight to my chest.

"Yeah, well there is no way I am going to thank you for having no balls," I said as I grabbed my purse and left.

FIVE

I drove home so fast I got not one but two speeding tickets. The first one while still on the island of Zealand, the other while hurrying toward the ferry because I didn't want to have to wait till the next one twenty minutes later. This trip had turned out to be quite expensive and so not worth my time.

As I stood on the deck of the ferry and watched my misty island approach in the distance, I finally managed to calm down. How I loved this strange little place in the middle of the North Sea. A woman came up to me with eyes wide and a book in her hand.

"Are you Emma Frost?"

I nodded. She held out a pen, and I signed her copy of *Itsy Bitsy Spider*, the first book I had ever written.

"I love your books. I have all of them," she said. "We actually decided to visit Fanoe island because of your books. I can't believe I actually got to meet you, the real Emma Frost. You're an amazing writer. Don't ever stop writing books. I'll keep reading as long as you write."

I felt a little emotional and sniffled. "I won't," I said. "I promise." As the woman left, smiling from ear to ear, I realized I wasn't going to let some publishing house stop me from getting my books out to my many readers. There had to be another way I could get this story out, a way that was easier.

The ferry arrived at the shore, and I drove off, feeling empowered and strong, while an idea lingered in the back of my head. I drove up to my beach house and got out, then walked inside. The smell of newly baked rolls filled my nostrils. In the kitchen, I found my mom and dad reading the paper together while holding hands. I had asked them to be at the house to keep an eye on Skye and be there when Victor got back, in case I didn't get there in time. Victor wouldn't be happy that I wasn't there as he loathed change, but he loved my dad and, as long as he got his afternoon tea as usual, then I believed we could avoid him having a tantrum. It took a while to explain to my mom that he wasn't just a spoiled twelve-year-old, but that he had a developmental condition, even though I didn't have a diagnosis for him.

"Emma? You're back?" my dad said, looking at me above his glasses.

"That was quick," my mom said. "Did everything go all right at the publishing house?"

I sighed and threw my manuscript on the counter. "They won't publish it. Is Victor home yet?"

"Not yet," my dad said.

"And Skye?"

"She's in the living room, waiting for him," my mom said, and then added, "What do you mean they won't publish it?"

I shrugged, grabbed myself a cup of coffee, and sipped it.

"They didn't like it, I guess."

"Well, it is quite different from your other books," my mom said. I had let them both read it because I needed their feedback, plus I really wanted them to know these things, to know what had happened and what Victor and Skye were capable of.

I knew my mom didn't like it much, even though she didn't say it directly. She just had a hard time picturing all these things.

"I never had much of an imagination," she said.

"But it's real, Mom," I tried to explain. "Victor does these things. It happened. All of it."

"Now, well... I don't know about that." she replied, making a face that told me she didn't believe me at all.

My dad was struggling with it too, but he seemed more open. He always believed Victor was quite special and not just an undisciplined child like my mom thought.

"We baked," my mom said, smiling. "Just like you wanted us to, to make sure Victor got the bread he usually gets when he gets home from that... place."

"School, Mom. We call it school, even though it is at a psychiatric institution."

"Oh, yes, well..."

I looked at the cooker and the rolls inside of it. "I think you need to get them out. They look a little brown to me."

My mom sprang to her feet. "Oh, dear Lord."

She opened the cooker and pulled out the rolls, then smiled. "They're only a little burnt."

I was about to say something just as I heard the school bus from Fishy Pines arrive in my driveway, and I ran out to greet Victor instead.

SIX

He hoped he could sneak in without her waking up. Brian Mortensen fumbled with the keys to open the front door. The Uber behind him left as he finally managed to step inside. The house was so quiet. Brian sighed deeply and took off his tie, then kicked off his shoes. He exhaled as he put down his briefcase next to his shoes, thinking about Jonna, the woman he had met with tonight while his wife thought he was working late.

It was all his coworker Carl's doing. Setting them up. Carl had done this for ten years, and his wife had never found out. For Carl it had all begun with a fling at a Christmas party... it was a cliché, yes, but the truth, nonetheless. Carl had told Brian about it in detail, how this very attractive senior member of the staff (he didn't want to mention any names, but Brian knew very well who she was) was being very seductive.

"She was all over me, being like, 'Oh, there's no one else in the building,'" Carl had explained. And then they had sex in her office.

It wasn't the fact that they had sex or the fact that Carl was having an affair that was so interesting about this story. No, what had made Brian listen extra carefully was when Carl talked about what had happened afterward. The sex was the fun part, of course, but there had been a side effect to it, an unexpected one, that held Brian's interest.

Once Carl had come home after the party, he had been so overwhelmed with guilt, he had made love to his wife the next morning in a way they never had before, attending to her every need in a manner that revitalized their sex life and their entire marriage.

That was why Carl did it, he had told Brian. He had affairs that usually never lasted more than a few months at a time. They would mostly meet up in some hotel room, and he would get to try all the things his wife wouldn't let him, and then he would go back home feeling so incredibly guilty that it made him be the best husband he could ever be. Plus, the secrecy, the knowledge that he was keeping this big secret from his wife, made it very erotic to him, arousing even. It was a rush he kept going back for more of. Just like a drug.

"It's incredible," Carl had told Brian a couple of months ago. "You should try it."

Brian had thought about it. A lot. His marriage was suffering and had been for a very long time. Especially since Ann got laid off—or forced to retire early as they liked to put it. Ann used to be this sexy woman whom he couldn't keep his hands off, but now she was doubting herself and feeling worthless in a way that made her not want to have sex with her husband.

It had been going on for so long that Brian was getting desperate. He had tried to explain to her that he had needs too, that he needed the closeness, but she kept pushing him away. And, on top of it all, there was the matter of her growing paranoia that drove him crazy. Ann kept hearing sounds and kept telling him she believed someone was following her. She tried to hide the fact that she was taking pills for it, but he had found them hidden behind the tampon box in the bathroom. He had no hope of getting her back to normal anytime soon.

Soon, he began to consider Carl's proposition and, weeks after he had told him about it, Brian was sitting in his office while Carl created a profile on Ashley Madison, the place where he could meet his next fling, as Carl liked to put it. It was apparently this dating website where you could chat with women who were looking for the same as you. Nothing but casual sex.

"Make sure you only chat with those who are already married. This is crucial. They need to be like you. Otherwise, they'll get clingy and start to ask you what you're doing and why you're seeing other women and text you during the day, and you don't want that," Carl had explained as they scrolled through the many women. Brian had never in his wildest imagination pictured himself meeting some woman through a website and then having sex with her just like that.

Was it really that easy?

As it turned out, it was. Brian soon started to chat with this woman and would stay at the office for hours after everyone else had left and chat with her online. The chatting soon turned into them wanting to meet up, and tonight had been the night.

But much to Brian's surprise—or disappointment—the sex hadn't been great. It had been awkward and clumsy, and he hadn't enjoyed a minute of it. He kept comparing this woman to Ann and quickly realized that she fell short. At one point, he had even found himself fantasizing that this woman was, in fact, his wife.

Now that he had tried it, Brian didn't feel quite the way he had thought he would. As he walked up the stairs toward their bedroom, he did feel guilty, as he had expected, but he didn't really feel that other part that Carl had talked about. The erotic part, the part where you feel almost high on an adrenaline rush and want to do it all over again.

All he felt was the guilty part. A deep disgust with himself for having done the unthinkable to his wife and all he could think about was that he would never ever want to do anything like this again.

Brian stood in front of the door to their bedroom and placed his hand on the doorknob, feeling like the worst husband in the world. He sighed and opened the door, wondering if he was ever going to be able to live with himself after this. Was he ever going to be able to look his wife in the eyes again?

Maybe I should just tell her everything.

It was against everything that Carl had advised him, but Brian knew it was the only thing he could do. If Ann left him, then so be it. He was the one who had screwed up by listening to an idiot like Carl. How could he have been so stupid? Brian and Ann had something unique. So many years together were truly special, and now he had destroyed it all.

Luckily, the kids were all grown and had left the house, so they wouldn't suffer from it, at least not as much as they would have had they still lived at home.

Maybe she'll just laugh at it with me when I tell her how awful it was. Maybe we can laugh at it together.

Brian shook his head. He knew his wife very well. She was going to be terribly angry with him because of this. But she might be able to forgive him... in time. At least, he hoped she would.

She might when she sees how sorry I am.

Brian walked into the bedroom, not turning the lights on. He took off his trousers, and then realized he was standing in some kind of water, his socks getting soaked. Brian sighed, thinking it was that darn toilet that had leaked again, then finally turned the light on to size up the damage. He felt annoyed at the prospect of having to spend yet another huge amount of money on a plumber and probably a new toilet.

If I had only listened to what he told me last time and

changed the toilet out for a newer model, this wouldn't have happened.

"Hope you have a canoe," the bastard plumber had said when he left.

As the light turned on and Brian looked at his wife, he knew immediately something was wrong. And not just because of the water on the floor. As he stared gaping at his wife's wide-open eyes, he also knew a simple *I'm sorry* wasn't going to cut it. There would be no relief, no laughing at how stupid this whole thing had been. He was going to be eaten up with guilt for the rest of his miserable life.

SEVEN

"Alexander is totally into you. Why don't you want to go out with him?"

Maya sighed and looked at her friend. Christina had been on her case about Alexander for weeks now, but Maya kept telling her she didn't want to date him, or anyone for that matter.

"I want to focus on school," she said. "We only have six months left, and I want to keep my grades up."

"Yeah, right," Christina said and sat up on Maya's bed. It was Sunday, and Christina had slept over.

Maya looked at her friend. "It's the truth."

"So, can't you both date someone and get good grades? That's ridiculous," she said.

Maya sighed and looked at her phone. The truth was that she had decided not to date anyone. Not after she lost both Asgar, her best friend who was madly in love with her, and Samuel who... well, that was a whole different story, but he too was gone, at least she hoped he was. She hadn't seen it for herself, but her mom had assured her he was dead.

Maya had been in love with Samuel, and she had almost

ended up getting herself and her brother killed. It had broken her heart that he turned out to be who he was and, to be honest, she didn't really trust anyone anymore. It was a whole strange story, and she didn't want Christina to know anything about it. She probably wouldn't understand it anyway.

"Come on," Christina said. "Just go out with him once. Just one time and then tell me you didn't enjoy it. If you don't do it because you like him, then do it just to look at him. He's so yummy!"

"Sounds like you should go out with him instead," Maya said and got out of the bed.

Outside the window, the garden was dressed completely in white. She could see Victor playing with his new friend Skye between the trees. If they were, in fact, playing. It seemed very quiet to be that. They were both sitting in front of the tall trees, eyes closed, legs in a lotus position, looking like they were meditating, backs turned against each other.

"What are they doing?" Christina asked, looking over Maya's shoulder. Maya sighed and shook her head.

"I honestly don't know."

Those kids were so weird, Maya couldn't even begin to explain it to Christina. The way they were constantly talking to each other without opening their mouths and letting out any sound, and then there was the matter of them lifting things by the power of their minds alone.

I have the weirdest family in the world.

There was a light knock on the door, and Maya's mom peeked inside.

"Good morning, girls. Sleep well?"

"Yes, Miss Frost," Christina said, sounding perky.

Maya's mom smiled. "Good. Breakfast is already on the table downstairs. The rest of us ate earlier, but we thought we'd let you two sleep in. Help yourself to anything you need. I'll be in my study."

"Okay, Mom," Maya said, hoping she would just go away before she said something embarrassing. Her mom had just written a book about Samuel and all that had happened to them, and Maya had begged her not to publish it because she didn't want everything that went on in her life to be public. Even though her mother changed the names in the book, people would still know it was her, she believed.

Fortunately, her publisher had told her the company didn't want to publish it, and Maya had been very thrilled about that, even though it upset her mother visibly. This story was just a little too close to home, she thought. She didn't want her friends to start realizing just how weird her family was. That was why she usually asked Christina if they could sleep over at her house instead, but for some reason, Christina was so fascinated by Maya's mom, because she was a writer and famous and all that, that she always begged Maya to have the sleepover at her house.

"We will. Thank you, Miss Frost," Christina said. "Say... are you working on anything interesting lately?"

Christina had read all of Emma Frost's books, and often she would ask Maya tons of questions about them, especially about the characters and what was going to happen to them. It would annoy Maya greatly. Christina was her mom's number one fan.

"As a matter of fact, I am," her mom said.

Oh, great. Now she's gonna get all chatty and talk about the book that no one will publish.

"Oh, really? A new book is coming out soon, I presume," Christina said, clasping her hands together in excitement.

Maya exhaled. She almost rolled her eyes at her friend but wanted to remain polite.

Presume? You never use words like that.

Christina was just trying to impress Maya's mother. Maya knew she was, and most other kids might have found it fun that their friends adored their mothers so much, but not Maya. She didn't want to have to wonder if they were friends with her because of her famous mother or because they liked her.

Maya's mom thought it over for a few seconds before answering.

Please don't give her the whole speech about the publishing house being idiots and having no balls. Please, don't.

"Well, yes. I am working on getting it published soon, I think."

"Really?" Christina was almost shrieking when she spoke. "Well, let me know when it comes out. I want to be the first to read it."

"Will do," her mom said. "I just need to—"

"Okay, I think it's time for us to get some breakfast," Maya said and signaled her mom to stop. She could tell she was about to start talking about her troubles getting the book published. She had that look in her eyes.

"I'm starving and so is Christina. We should really get something to eat."

"Oh, okay," her mom said. "Sure. As I said, there's bread on the table and butter and cheese in the fridge."

"We'll probably just grab some yogurt and fruit," Maya said.

"Really?" her mom said. "The bread is really good, though. I put sunflower seeds in it this time."

"Sounds delicious," Christina said. "I think I would like some of that."

"Well, help yourselves to whatever you want," Maya's mom said. "I have work to do."

"Break a leg," Christina yelled after her as she was about to leave.

Maya grimaced.

Break a leg?

Maya's mom paused, then smiled politely. "Thank you... I guess."

EIGHT

I had an idea. A plan almost. I didn't know if it was going to work, but I wanted to try at least. I wasn't going to just sit there in my house and mope over the fact that my publishing house wasn't going to take on my book. Nope. It wasn't my style. I wasn't going to send it to another publishing house either. I was sick of publishers and editors telling me what to do and especially what not to do.

It was easier than I had thought it would be. I had asked a friend of mine, who was a graphic designer, to create a cover for me, then opened a web page. I uploaded my manuscript to it, then set a price and pressed PUBLISH. The web page told me the book was now in review and that it would take twenty-four hours before it would be available for sale in the online shop.

Just like that.

All my other books were already available as e-books in the same online shop, so after I formatted it, I didn't really have to do anything else, not even create an author profile. I stared at the screen, wondering if anyone would ever realize it was out there.

I had to take advantage of the fact that I was already a

household name. If I wanted this book to be seen and read, there were ways of doing that. I knew people in the media business all over the country, so I wrote emails to all of them, sending them an electronic copy of my book. I explained that I had decided to self-publish it because no one else dared to publish it because it was controversial and that I hoped they might do a little feature or write a note about it in their paper.

I closed my computer, feeling pretty good about myself, found my box of macadamia nut biscuits in the drawer, and started to eat. The biscuits were like a week old and tasted stale, but I still ate them. Morten had been on my case lately, trying to get me to lose weight. He was monitoring what I ate and trying to "help" me by asking me if I "really wanted to eat that." My mom soon chimed in, and that meant I could hardly eat anything without one of them—or sometimes both of them—watching me and commenting on my choices. It was very annoying, to be honest.

It was all Dr. Williamsen's fault for telling me I had high blood pressure. And my own for telling my family about it when coming home from my checkup. And my mom's fault. Yes, it was definitely mostly her. She was the one who had told me I should start doing yearly checkups. But after this experience, I wasn't going to go again next year, that was for sure. I would agree to do decadal checkups if there was such a thing. But not every freakin' year. Nope. Wasn't doing it.

I was probably just agitated when he took my blood pressure, I decided. I did feel a little wound up because I was nervous and all. Checkups were scary. I was terrified he would come back out and tell me I had three months to live because of some lump I had failed to discover on my own.

It was so my mother's fault, I thought while chewing my biscuit. I had hidden chocolate and snacks all over the house and was eating in secret now, which made it less fun. It made me feel like a child.

It was only when Sophia dropped by that I could eat with no guilt because she ate along with me. She wasn't big like me though, and she didn't have high blood pressure, which I now envied her tremendously. I guessed that having six kids kept her on her toes constantly and that was why she was so fit. I didn't envy her that part. Having Skye in the house had made my life easier, but I wasn't going to have any more children. I was done with that part, thank you very much. My babies were my books now, and I had just sent one of them into the world to see if it would fly. It was ridiculous how I felt a lot more nervous about this one than the many others I had written.

NINE

"I'm sorry I'm late."

Morten leaned down and kissed my cheek. I was sitting at the dinner table with my parents and all three children when he walked in. Morten's seat had remained empty all throughout the meal.

"The phone has been invented," my mother said.

I gave her a look to quiet her. She was right, though; Morten should have called and told me he would be late, but if anyone was going to say anything, it had to be me and not her. Not that I was going to. It wasn't like we were married or even lived together. He had told me he would stop by for dinner, but I knew he could get held up at work. It happened.

"Let me heat up a pork chop and some mashed potatoes for you," I said and went into the kitchen. I filled his plate with food, then nuked it before I returned. Morten gave me a tired smile.

"Thanks, sweetie."

I sat down, then grabbed a cold pork chop and ate it while Morten shoveled down his food. Now it was my mother's turn to give me a look.

"What? I can't let the poor man eat alone," I said. "I'm just being polite and trying to make him feel comfortable."

"You don't have to," Morten said, chewing a mouthful. "I don't mind eating alone."

"You really shouldn't—" my mom started, but my dad put a hand on top of hers to make her stop. She looked at him. "She's got high blood pressure for cryin' out loud. She should lose weight."

I rolled my eyes at her, then gulped down another bite, feeling like a rebellious teenager. Maya gave me a look, then sighed like I was the most embarrassing person in the world, which I admit I probably was.

Luckily, her friend had returned to her own house after the sleepover. I liked Christina, especially because she was such a good friend to Maya, but I couldn't stand how she was constantly all over me. I knew Maya hated it too. It had to be annoying for her.

"So, tell us, Morten, why are you late?" my dad asked, trying to change the subject. He was my accomplice in all this, my only helper whenever Morten and my mom ganged up on me.

Morten hooked a piece of pork on his fork, then ate it. "We had to respond to a death."

"What?" I asked, quickly turning my head.

"Yeah, it's quite disturbing actually," Morten said with a sigh. "You remember the Mortensens from Granvej? Brian and Ann? We met them last year at a dinner party. He worked for that shipping company on the mainland, and she worked for that research lab, the one out of town."

"Omicon? Yeah, I remember them. Nice couple. Did something happen to them?" I asked.

"She's dead," he said, nodding.

"What? How?"

"We don't know that yet," Morten said. "But according to

Brian, he came home in the middle of the night and found her in the bed. Dead."

"Was she... killed?"

Morten shook his head. "We don't think so, no. It looked like she just died in her sleep. Probably a heart attack. The autopsy will let us know later this week, hopefully."

I clasped my mouth. "Oh, dear God. Poor Brian."

Morten nodded. "I know."

"Yeah, maybe now you'll understand why it's important to keep your heart healthy," my mom chirped.

"I have a little high blood pressure," I said angrily. "Half of the population has high blood pressure. It's not like I'm going to die."

"And cholesterol," my mom added. "Don't forget about that. Besides, I bet that Ann character said the same and look what happened to her."

"Would you let it go already?" I snapped.

I had regretted so many times telling her what Dr. Williamsen had said. It was so stupid of me, but back then, I hadn't thought she would turn this into a big deal and be on my case all the time. I was a little surprised myself and just wanted to get it off my chest. Now she insisted on stuffing it back in over and over again, filling me with guilt.

"Please... Ulla," my dad said. "Can't we just have a nice family dinner for once?"

My mom rose to her feet, her plate between her hands. "I am just concerned for my daughter's well-being. Is that a crime now?"

"No, Mom, that is not a crime, but..." I sighed and rubbed my forehead while my mom snorted and left for the kitchen without waiting for me to finish my sentence. My dad got up and followed her. He kissed me on the forehead.

"We'll probably head home, sweetie. Mom is tired."

"Thanks for coming over, Dad," I said while he blew finger

kisses at the children. Maya had already left the table, her face probably red in embarrassment, while Victor and Skye were sitting eerily quiet, staring into each other's eyes, probably sharing all kinds of secrets between them. I couldn't quite figure out if their relationship was healthy or not. In the beginning, I had believed Skye had gotten Victor out of his shell a little, but as the days passed, it seemed like she was dragging him more and more into her world, a world none of us could enter, while Victor became increasingly distant to me. Was it just him growing up? Or was it unhealthy for him?

I heard the front door slam as my parents left, then looked at Morten, who had grabbed a beer from the kitchen.

"Can you believe her?" I said. "How inappropriate of her. To use Ann Mortensen's tragedy like that for her little vendetta against me. Like that had anything to do with me."

Morten didn't say anything. He drank his beer.

"You agree with her, don't you?" I said.

He looked at me, tired. "Why won't you listen to what the doctor says?"

"Great. Take her side. That's perfect, Morten," I said, grabbed the pan in front of me and walked out to the kitchen with it. Morten didn't follow me but stayed in the dining room drinking his beer.

TEN

Next morning, I sent Victor off, with the school bus taking him to Fishy Pines while Maya took care of getting herself to the secondary school on her own. It had snowed heavily all night, so she couldn't ride her bike, but the school was so close that she decided to walk instead.

I tried to kiss her before she left, but she brushed me off and rushed out the door. I stood in the kitchen and looked after her, my favorite cup between my hands. On the side it read I DON'T NEED TO DEAL WITH REALITY. I AM A WRITER. Maya had bought it for me on my birthday, and I loved it.

I stared at Maya fighting her way through the snow, then thought about myself when I was her age. Gosh, I had hated my mother. I guessed I should count myself lucky that Maya at least tolerated me. And every now and then, we actually had a good and nice conversation with no rolling of eyes or deep sighs. But those days were rarer now than they used to be.

I walked upstairs to my office and sat down by my computer when suddenly my phone started to ring. Praying it wasn't Victor's school telling me something had happened, I picked it up. It wasn't Fishy Pines. It was my publisher.

"What have you done?"

"Well, hello to you too, Inger," I said.

"Quit it. I'm being serious here, Emma. What the heck have you done? Why would you do such a thing?"

"Are you referring to my book and the fact that I have self-published it?" I asked, sipping my coffee. I was quite surprised that Inger was already reacting to this. I had just put it up the day before and hadn't even seen if it was out yet. But apparently, it was.

"Why would you do this to yourself? To your brand?" Inger asked.

To my brand. Yes, of course, that's how she saw me. As a brand, a product.

"Listen, Inger. I know you didn't wasn't to publish it, so I decided to do this instead. At least I didn't take it to another publishing house. You should be happy I didn't do that."

Inger exhaled. "Emma, I am talking to you as a friend here, not your publisher. Do you have any idea what you have done to yourself? To your books? To you as an author?"

Now it was my turn to exhale. "No, Inger, I don't. And, frankly, I don't care. This book is my heart. I have to get it out to my readers."

"Readers who have always seen you as a true crime writer, as someone who wrote wonderful mysteries based on real events. Now, what are they supposed to believe?"

"I put it in as fiction, okay? Supernatural fiction."

"But that's not what your audience is expecting from you, Emma."

"So, it's something new," I said, not really understanding what the fuss was about. It was just a book. "They might love it."

"So, I'm taking it you haven't read the newspapers this morning?" Inger asked.

"I haven't, no," I said, feeling a little nervous now.

"Maybe you should. Then let's talk about how to do some damage control for your brand."

ELEVEN

They hated it. They all hated my book. I couldn't believe my own eyes as I read through the many reviews posted in all the national newspapers in the country. I had sent them a copy of the book, yes, but I had never in my wildest imagination thought they would actually read it. I guess I had underestimated my own status or brand or whatever they want to call it.

Apparently, me deciding to self-publish a book was headline news. But not the good kind. It was the kind where they told me I wasn't doing myself any favors by not listening to my publisher and that there was a reason the publishing house rejected the book. It was simply not worth the reader's time.

They really didn't like it.

I didn't understand. I was never one to receive applause or awards for my writing, but the last couple of books I had written had received decent reviews, and I was beginning to consider myself to be quite good. But now this? Was Inger really right about the book?

Feeling sorry for myself, I walked back down to the kitchen and poured myself another cup of coffee, then found my secret stash of chocolate chip biscuits behind the cereal boxes in the cabinet and dug in while looking at the falling snow outside my window. It was pretty but merciless.

As I lost myself in my thoughts, I suddenly spotted Sophia fighting her way through the thick curtain of snowflakes toward my house. I hurried to the door and opened it for her, so she could get in.

"Thanks," she said and stomped her feet to let the snow fall off on my floor where it soon melted and became a puddle. "It's nasty out."

"Tell me about it," I said and helped her get her jacket off, then put it on a hanger where it could dry. Sophia had snow in her hair and brushed it off. Realizing someone was here (as always, way too late), Kenneth came storming out, barking aggressively at her.

"Easy Kenneth Two," I said. "It's just Sophia, even though she does look like a yeti."

"Brrr," Sophia said and swung her arms to get warmer. "You got the fireplace going?"

"Not yet, but now I will," I said and walked into the living room, while Kenneth threw himself at Sophia's shoes and, realizing this, Sophia grabbed them, and they started a tug-of-war till the dog finally let go. I put wood in the fireplace and lit it, then looked at Sophia.

"How about some hot chocolate?" I asked.

"Sounds great."

I warmed up two cups for us and put whipped cream on top along with a giant marshmallow, then walked back to Sophia with the cups between my hands. When Sophia saw them, she gave me a look.

"Marshmallow, huh? What's going on? Are you and Morten fighting? Or is it Maya? Or Victor? Is something up with Victor at the school? Don't tell me they've thrown him out too."

"No, that's not it."

"Phew, because I wouldn't know where you'd put him after that. Fishy Pines is the last resort, if you know what I mean."

I ignored her remark. I was becoming increasingly happy with Fishy Pines and the work HP was doing with Victor. I didn't know if he was actually learning anything, but he didn't seem to get himself into as much trouble as he did in the regular school, and they hadn't talked about medicating him at all, much to my surprise.

"Then, what's up?" Sophia asked and sipped her hot chocolate.

When she moved the cup from her mouth, a smear of whipped cream was left on the tip of her nose.

I grabbed my iPad and showed her an article in a newspaper. My picture was above it. Sophia read, "The self-published *Waltzing Matilda* is undeniably news in the world of books. Unfortunately, it is bad news. There are two equally serious reasons why this book isn't worth any reader's attention. The first is that it is dull. Dull in a pretentious, florid, and archly fatuous fashion. The second is that it is repulsive..."

Sophia stopped herself and put the iPad down. "Oh."

"I know." I sipped my own hot chocolate while staring into the fire.

"So, you self-published. Was it because Inger didn't want to publish it?" Sophia asked.

"Yes. It seemed like a great idea at the time. Now, they're all speculating that I think I'm better than everyone else and that, from now on, I'll just be one of those self-published authors who couldn't get their books published by a real publishing house and so on. Because I refused to accept the fact that my book isn't good enough."

"But isn't that the truth?" Sophia asked. "That you self-published it because no one else would."

"This is a good book. I love it, and I wanted my readers to read it and love it too."

"But it's so different," Sophia said. "People have come to expect a certain type of book from you, and this... well, it's not the same."

"I still think it's good," I said with a sigh.

Sophia put a hand on my shoulder. "I think it's good too. I really like it. You know I do. What do you care what everyone else thinks? If you're proud of it, then so be it. You should be."

"Do you think I should take it down?" I asked.

"And let them win? Never! The book is out there, and there is nothing you can do about that. If you take it down, they'll think they were right. You won't hear the end of it. It's like kids. You can never let them think they are right."

I nodded. My marshmallow had become gooey from the warm chocolate milk, just the way I liked it.

"Okay," I said. "I'll leave it up."

"Just stay away from reviews and newspapers from now on. And don't google yourself anymore. I know you say you don't do that, but I know you do. Stop it. Don't read any of the nonsense they're writing. And no social media. Don't read emails either. Just stop going on your computer and enjoy your family instead. Maybe write a new book. Do you have any new ideas?"

"Not really," I said and looked into the fire. After the reviews I had spent the morning reading, I wasn't sure I even wanted to write anymore. It was going to be very hard getting back up on that horse again.

TWELVE

"Omigosh! Alexander is wearing that red sweater today. It makes him look sooo yummy."

Maya looked at Christina, then glanced at Alexander at the table next to them where he was sitting with all his friends eating their lunch. As he sensed her eyes on him, he lifted his head and smiled at her. She didn't smile back.

"He's so into you, Maya. You have to do something about it. You have to go out with him."

Maya shook her head. "I don't have to do anything. I'm fine where I am. I told you."

Maya looked down at her algebra book. She had a test later today and wanted to read up for it. She thought she heard Christina shriek, then lifted her head again and realized Alexander was standing right in front of her. Her heart dropped.

"Hi," he said.

Maya finally smiled, but only to be polite. The last thing she wanted was for him to think she was into him. She kind of was; she thought he was really cute, but she didn't want to be. She wanted to finish school and move on.

"Hey, there."

Alexander sat down across from her. "I saw you riding your bike through downtown this weekend."

"Really?" she said, unimpressed.

He looked at his fingers. "And I was wondering if maybe one day you and I... could... bike downtown together. Maybe to see a film or get something to eat. Or how about this Saturday you and I bike to Thomas K's party together?"

And there it was. The question she had dreaded would come. She had prepared for it, but it was always harder when she actually sat in front of the person. Especially because this person was so cute and, had things been different, if it hadn't been for what she went through with Samuel, then, well... she would probably have said yes.

"I don't think so," Maya said, her eyes returning to the book.

Please, go away now. Please.

Alexander's friends made noises in the background, and someone yelled. "Ouch."

Maya didn't look at him till after he got up. She felt heartbroken and lifted her gaze to watch him walk away.

In another lifetime maybe.

"You turned him down?" Christina could hardly breathe.

Maya closed her book. "I told you I would."

"But why? He's so hot!"

"I told you. I need to focus on school."

Maya grabbed her book and held it against her chest, then rushed out of the cafeteria, feeling devastated yet determined. Alexander was cute, yes, but she didn't want to go down that road again. She simply didn't dare. If Christina couldn't understand that, then, well... that was her problem.

THIRTEEN

I tried my best; I really, honestly did. I baked a ton of biscuits, then prepared a pie for dessert tonight, while getting the roast ready and marinating the potatoes. I listened to music while cooking, whistling along, trying hard to push all the bad thoughts away and not wonder what else people were writing about me online.

And, much to my surprise, I succeeded. I managed to go all day without opening my computer, checking emails, or looking at social media, and I even let the voicemail handle my many phone calls. Most of them were from journalists who wanted a comment on the bad reviews and on my decision to self-publish, but I deleted them as fast as they arrived.

At two-thirty, Skye came down from upstairs and rushed toward the front door. I knew then that Victor was almost home and, just as I suspected, the school bus drove up less than a second later.

He came up to the house, and I opened the door to greet him, but he completely ignored me and rushed toward Skye. They hugged, and I felt so jealous I screamed inside of me. I hadn't been able to touch my son for years and here she was, hugging him. Just wrapping her arms around him and holding him tight. And he didn't scream. He didn't even complain.

I should be happy that my son was socializing with other kids, letting them come close to him and actually touch him; I know I should, but I was just so... jealous. I missed holding my boy.

"Afternoon tea in thirty minutes," I yelled after them as they rushed into the living room. I knew they would be playing in the garden in only a few seconds, talking to the trees or whatever weird stuff they did out there.

I followed them, then noticed that both of them had stopped in front of the bathroom door. Both small bodies stood like they were frozen, staring at the closed door.

"What's going on?" I asked. "Aren't you going to the garden?"

That was when I noticed that Brutus, Victor's strange and very quiet pit bull was also sitting there, glaring at the door, like he expected someone to come out of it.

"Victor?"

He didn't move. I noticed his hands were shaking as he stood there staring at the door.

"Vic? What's going on? Skye?"

But no one paid any attention to me. They just stood there, completely paralyzed, looking at the darn door like they expected it to open or something, but nothing happened.

I knew Victor often believed that bathrooms were evil for some reason and avoided them at school, but I had never seen him react to them at home. I had always believed it was just his way of telling me he didn't like school or something like that. Maybe someone had beaten him up or bullied him in some way inside one of the bathrooms, and he just didn't want to tell me.

"Victor. It's just our bathroom. You go past it every day," I said, trying to talk some sense into the boy. Then I sighed, walked to the door, and opened it, wanting to show them that there was absolutely nothing to be afraid of.

"See?" I said and walked inside.

And that was when I heard it. A loud slithering sound, like a big snake or something disappearing down the drain of the bathtub. I grabbed the curtain and pulled it aside. Whatever it was, it moved so fast I couldn't see it.

I shrieked and hurried back out, then closed the door, heart throbbing in my chest.

"Okay. That's it. I'm calling in the experts."

FOURTEEN

Sven Thomsen loathed his neighbor more than anything in this world. While shoveling snow outside his own house, Sven threw a glare toward the neighbor's sidewalk. Just this morning, Sven had stopped his neighbor as he rushed for his car, a cup of coffee clutched in his hand.

Always so busy, busy, busy. Doesn't even have time to drink his coffee because he's so darn busy all the time. Always on the go with that stupid coffee in his hand. Why doesn't anyone have time just to sit down and drink their coffee anymore? Why must they take it everywhere, always on the go-go-go?

Sven didn't care much that his neighbor was in a hurry. He had rushed out to him, wearing big boots underneath his robe, then yelled at him. "Hey. Wait a minute."

The neighbor had paused with a sigh. "What now, Sven? I have a meeting at eight."

"You still have half an hour. That's plenty of time," Sven had told him. "When I was your age, I drove to—"

"I don't really have time for your stories, Sven. What do you want?" The neighbor had cut him off.

Sven had grunted, annoyed. Again with the busyness, never time to even listen to people. What if Sven had something important to tell him? Some deep advice that could change his perspective on life. But, oh, no, the young of today have no time for that because they're so darn BUSY!

"I just wanted to remind you that you have to shovel the snow on the sidewalk. It's the law, you know."

The neighbor exhaled and looked at his watch for the fifth time during their brief conversation.

"I know, Sven. You told me that last month too when it snowed."

"Aha, but you didn't do it, remember? And there was a lady walking through it who almost fell. Can't have that, can we? Must obey the law. That's why it's there. No one is above it."

"All right," the neighbor said. "I'll take care of it. Now, if you'll excuse me, I have an important meeting to attend."

Important meeting. A meeting was never just a meeting anymore. It was always *important.*

"Very well," Sven had said. "But if it is not cleared this afternoon, then I see no other way than to call the police."

The neighbor had been halfway inside his BMW by that point.

"See you later, Sven," was his answer before he took off.

Now, Sven was standing on the sidewalk. It was afternoon, and the neighbor's part of it was still covered in snow. Sven knew the neighbor wouldn't be home till late tonight when it was already dark out.

Sven hissed, annoyed, then walked back toward his own house. By now, he had shoveled snow twice already today. It was the duty as a homeowner, and he couldn't for the life of him understand why people didn't take these things more seriously.

Inside his house, he grabbed his phone with the intention of calling the number of the local police, but as he pushed a button to get his darn phone to light up, there was a noise coming from his bathroom, one that made him forget the phone, forget about sidewalks and law-breaking neighbors and walk toward the open door instead.

FIFTEEN

It was nice and quiet outside the school when Maya rushed out after the end of her last class. It was still snowing but not as much as this morning. Maya loved how the snow subdued everything and made her feel like she was standing inside her own dome and not having all the noises from the world disturb her. Ever since she had experienced her memory loss, something else had happened to Maya that she didn't talk to her mom about. She heard things differently, louder in some way that she couldn't really explain. And she was so sensitive to them.

Noises annoyed her greatly. Like when people ate, she could get almost aggressive toward them if they made the smallest noise. Even in class when the girl sitting next to her swallowed too loudly or played with her plastic water bottle, it made Maya's toes crumple with irritation. Sometimes, she would run to the restroom and hold her ears just to make the noises of the world go quiet for a few seconds, so she could relax. It was quite exhausting.

She knew her brother was sensitive to noises, and there were days when she wondered if she was becoming more and more like him. Maybe she just found it difficult to think straight when there was too much noise. Because there was so much noise inside her mind.

"Hey... wait up, Maya!"

The silence was broken by a familiar voice. Maya sighed and turned to look at him.

"Alex, hey..."

"Are you walking home?" he asked.

She nodded. "Not really weather to be biking in."

"Same here. Can we walk together?"

She hesitated for a few seconds, wanting to say no because it was the smart thing to do, but there was something about the look in Alex's eyes that made her soft, made her not want to hurt him again.

"Sure."

His face lit up beneath the beanie, and they began to walk. It was only about a five-minute walk for her, so it couldn't be too bad. Besides, she kind of enjoyed his company. She was being very careful not to let him think she was into him in any way. Because she wasn't. She wouldn't let herself be. It was out of the question. The result was, she didn't say a word to him, and soon the silence between them felt awkward. After a minute or so of walking, Maya regretted her decision.

"So... will you be going to the party on Saturday?" he finally asked, after searching for the right words for a long time.

Maya shook her head. "I'm not really that into parties and stuff like that."

"Yeah, me either," he said.

It was a lie. Maya knew he liked to party. He was the type of boy who always went to every party there was.

"So... what do you like to do?" he asked, kicking a pile of snow on the side of the road.

"Read. Watch anime."

"Ah... I see," he said.

"Listen, Alex," she said when they stopped outside her house. "You're a nice guy and everything, but we don't really have much in common."

He looked so disappointed that she almost lost her courage. Did she really have to let him down twice in one day?

But the real problem wasn't that she had to let him down for the second time; the real issue occurred seconds later when Alex leaned over and kissed her.

Maya pulled away forcefully.

"What the heck are you doing?"

He gave her a look, one of confidence. "I know you like me. Let's stop the charade for a second. Just admit it."

Maya stared at him. Who the heck did he think he was?

"I... I... that's... not true."

He pointed at her with both his fingers, then started to walk away. "I got to kiss Maya Frost. I got to kiss Maya Frost."

"You did not... I wasn't even..."

But Alex was already gone. She could hear him whistling through the heavy curtain of snow long after she couldn't see him anymore.

SIXTEEN

I was in luck. Apparently, our local plumbing company had a plumber right down the street attending to another house when I called, and he had promised he could stop by my place when he was done there. So, ten minutes later, a small minivan drove up in my driveway and parked in the snow. I opened the door, and the plumber holding his toolbox walked up to my door, snowflakes on the top of his cap, where it said, PETERSEN PLUMBING—IF WATER RUNS THROUGH IT... WE DO IT!

"It's right in here," I said and walked ahead of him toward the guest bathroom. I was about to grab the handle and open the door but then didn't. Instead, I stepped aside.

"In there."

The plumber opened the door. Standing behind him, I watched as he walked in.

"The bathtub," I said.

"And what exactly is wrong with the bathtub?" he asked.

"There was something inside it. It disappeared down the drain when I pulled the curtain aside. But it was definitely there."

The plumber knelt down next to it with an exhale. "I can

take a look, but if it's an animal, I can't really do much about it," he grunted. "You'll need an exterminator. Is it clogged?"

"I... I don't know. I rarely use this one."

The plumber leaned forward and turned on the water, then watched to see if it ran down the drain with no trouble. It did.

"Seems fine to me," he said.

"But there was something there, down there..." I said and pointed.

"Has it been flooding?"

I shook my head.

The plumber rose to his feet, complaining, "Listen, lady. It could have been anything. Frogs, toads, snakes, maybe even a squirrel."

"A squirrel?" I asked, baffled.

He shrugged. "It's been known to happen. Believe it or not, some critters can crawl, creep, or wriggle their way into your pipes, causing clogs of all kinds. If you have an animal invasion, then it will probably start with a baffling flood and only end when you grab a broom and hysterically sweep the poor creature out the door."

"So, are you telling me I have some sort of critter down there? And that it came up through the drain and might even run into the house?" I shuddered at the thought.

"Yes, well, because there is no flooding or clogging, it can hardly be a big animal, if you want my opinion. Maybe just a frog. Maybe there's more than one."

"Frogs? I can live with frogs as long as they stay down there. A frog infestation sounds less appealing."

The plumber shrugged. "It's cold out. Lots of animals search for shelter in the pipes when it's cold. They might disappear on their own. Just wait and see."

The plumber grabbed his toolbox and walked back into the hallway. I wasn't sure I felt any better, maybe a little. As long as it was just frogs. A frog, preferably. One. Not multiple.

The plumber walked to the door and was about to open it when he spotted Victor's backpack on the floor. It was half open, and a book had slipped out of it. It had a sticker on the front of it stating, THIS BOOK BELONGS TO FISHY PINES. The plumber stared at it, then up at me.

"Is your kid at Fishy Pines?"

I nodded. "He goes to the school. He's not there full-time."

The plumber became distant, then nodded. "Okay. Good."

"What do you mean by that?"

He shook his head. "It's nothing. I just... well, I have a colleague, well, one I used to work with back in the eighties when we were both young. He went to a job there and disappeared. We've never heard from him since. He never made it home to his wife that night, and he didn't come to work the next morning. The minivan was still parked outside the building when we found it the next day."

"That's odd," I said.

"Yeah, a strange story, if you ask me. He was working in that old part, the condemned part of the building, back when it still housed patients. They had a lot of trouble back then with their pipes. Guess that's why it's condemned today, huh? The old building is probably falling apart."

"So, your friend was never found again."

"Nope." He shrugged again. "Ah, well... we all figured he just had enough of fixing everyone's toilets and ran off. Probably living on some Caribbean island somewhere, I reckon'."

"Sure sounds better," I said chuckling.

"Sure does. Can't help dreaming of sun and warmth at this time of year, can we now? You have a good day, ma'am. And call me if the drain clogs or anything like that. Watch out for flooding."

"Will do."

"And don't worry. These critters usually find their way out again after a little while, if they don't freeze to death when the pipes freeze over. Then you'll have a whole new set of problems once spring comes around. Nothing like the stench of a decaying animal."

"Let's just hope they come out before then," I said, then closed the door behind him as he walked back into the snow. I returned to the living room, walked past the bathroom door, then paused outside of it, putting my ear to the door to listen.

Nothing. Not even a drip.

"Frogs," I said with a scoff in the same second as Maya stormed inside the front door.

"Hey there, sweetie..." I said, but the girl just rushed past me and up the stairs without a word. She simply threw her backpack and shoes on the floor, then slammed the door to her room behind her.

SEVENTEEN

I decided to give Maya her space and went into the kitchen to prepare afternoon tea. It had to be ready at three o'clock, or it might throw Victor completely out of it. I rushed as much as I could, but at exactly three o'clock when Victor came into the kitchen, I wasn't ready.

Victor didn't care. He sat down at his chair, his head bent.

"Where's afternoon tea? It's three o'clock."

Skye sat next to him while Brutus loomed in the corner, looking more like a porcelain statue than a real live dog.

"I'm almost done, buddy," I said and took the warm bread out of the cooker.

"But it's three o'clock," he said.

"I know, but I had to take care of the plumber, remember?"

"Three o'clock is time for afternoon tea, just as six o'clock is dinner," he said. "That's the way it has always been."

I cut two pieces of bread, then put jam on them and served him, only two minutes late.

Victor stared at the floor, his nostrils flaring. I watched him, wondering if those nostrils would expand even farther and it would turn into a regular tantrum. But then I noticed Skye reach her hand over and place it on top of Victor's, and suddenly his shoulders relaxed, and he calmed down. A second later, he started to eat.

Wow.

I sat down too, enjoying a cup of coffee with my bread, and we all ate in silence while Skye played with the knife and let it dangle in the air in front of her. I pretended not to notice, because it was just the three of us, and sipped my coffee, wondering what kind of spell the girl had put on my son. Then, as I thought more about it, I realized that maybe my son was in fact just experiencing his first love, and my heart melted completely.

"So, how was school today?" I asked.

"Same," Victor said.

"No new friends?" I asked.

He didn't answer, and I guessed no.

Seconds later, when he was done eating, he got up and left the table.

"Hey, buddy," I yelled after him. "Wait for Skye. She's not done yet."

Skye smiled, then swallowed her last bite, and soon she joined him, holding his hand as they ran back into the garden after getting dressed in their winter snowsuits. I watched them for a few seconds when my phone rang again. I had decided not to pick it up but looked at the screen and then realized it was Victor's therapist.

"Hello," I said. "HP?"

"Hey there, Emma."

My heart dropped. Was he calling to tell me bad news? Had Victor done something at school today?

"What's wrong?" I asked.

"Nothing's wrong, Emma. No, on the contrary. I am calling to let you know that Victor has made a friend here. It's a step forward for him, so I thought I'd share it with you."

"A friend? But... but I just asked him if he made any new friends..."

"Well, you know how detailed oriented your son is, and to be honest, he isn't exactly a new friend as he's been here longer than Victor. But he is a friend."

"But... but that's good news."

"Yes, Emma. Your son is doing great. He has a wonderful mind. I don't think I've ever met anyone quite like him. I absolutely love working with him, and I think the fact that we do a few private lessons a week and then the rest in the class with the other kids is a good combination for him."

"A friend," I said, almost tearing up. "A real friend. And he's a boy. A boyfriend."

"Yes, Emma. His name is Daniel."

EIGHTEEN

It was quite a feast I had ended up preparing and, even though I was annoyed with my mom, I still invited both of my parents over to eat with Morten and me and the kids. Morten's daughter Jytte wasn't thrilled that he wasn't home for dinner again, so I invited her as well, even though I knew she hated me, but she said no.

I served the roast and the potatoes, feeling very proud of myself for not having been on the internet all day. The phone had been constantly ringing all afternoon, but now it had finally quieted down. Finally, those vultures understood that I wasn't going to talk to any of them. I didn't need them and their criticism or drama. I had everything I needed right here at my dinner table.

Maya poked her potato, then scooped it around a few times, her face long and her eyes not looking up at the rest of us. Skye and Victor were sitting quietly, staring into each other's eyes, and I had to constantly remind them to eat.

"Vegetables too, Victor," I told him.

They were holding hands under the table and thought I didn't notice. I couldn't figure out if it made me happy or sad. I was glad he had found someone in his life, someone he liked, but at the same time, he was still my little boy, right? Plus, I wasn't sure it was healthy for him, the way she monopolized him. He needed to interact more with his surroundings, with his family.

"So, Victor... I heard you've made a friend at school," I said. "HP called me and told me."

Victor didn't look at me.

"That's awesome, buddy," I continued.

"Why is that awesome?" he said.

"Because it's good for you to have a friend."

"I already have a friend. I have Skye."

"I know. I know," I said. "It's good to have many friends. And now you have one at school."

"Why do you keep stating the obvious?" he asked. "I know I have a friend at school."

"I just thought that maybe you'd like to invite him over one day, huh?" I asked.

But Victor had already lost interest in what I was saying. He and Skye were done eating and excused themselves and left. I looked after him, wondering what he shared with Skye that he never did with me.

My boy is happy. Don't make it an issue. Don't create a problem that isn't there.

I took another piece of meat and ate while wondering how to stop being jealous of my son's girlfriend. Was it typical to feel this way? I guessed it was. Maybe I just felt it a little more extreme because I never really felt like Victor was mine. I guess I was afraid of losing the little I had.

"So, Morten, any exciting news from your work?" my mom asked.

"Well, no, not really," he said, chewing. "The island had a pretty quiet day today, which is good."

"That is good," my dad said and put his silverware down.

"When the police are bored, things are going well for our community."

Morten scratched his forehead. "I wouldn't say I'm bored, but yes, you're absolutely right. It's one of the few professions that you really want to be out of work."

We finished our dinner and Morten helped me clean up while my mom and dad watched the news in the living room. I knew that my mom was itching to say something about my self-publishing ordeal, but I was surprised to see that she kept quiet all through dinner. I bet my dad had something to do with that.

I washed the dishes while Morten dried a pan. He looked at the water coming out of the tap.

"They say she drowned," he suddenly said, his eyes fixed on the water. I turned it off.

"What? Who... Ann?"

He nodded and put the pan down. "She had water inside her lungs. Her stomach was filled too. Several of her organs were so filled with water they had burst."

"What? That sounds crazy! How's that even possible?"

He shook his head. "I don't know. The forensic team says the water must have somehow been forced inside of her. It doesn't look like a typical drowning. It had to have happened fast too."

"So, do you think she was killed?"

He shrugged. "It can hardly have happened by accident, they said. But I don't know. It sounds very odd."

I stared into the sink where the water was slowly running down the drain, making a sucking sound as it disappeared.

"It sure does. I mean, how do you force water inside someone, use a pressure washer?"

Morten shrugged again. "I honestly don't know. It all sounds very odd to me, but again, I'm no expert."

I returned to my dishes, and we worked together in quiet, each of us wondering what had happened to poor Ann

Mortensen when my dad came out and told us they were heading home.

"Mom's tired."

"Thanks for coming over, Dad," I said and wiped my hands on the tea towel, then followed him back into the hallway to say goodbye. I kissed my dad on the cheek.

"Did you say goodbye to the kids?"

He nodded. "Don't worry about Maya," he said with a low voice.

"Boy trouble?" I asked, knowing my dad had a way of getting things out of my daughter that I never could.

He nodded. "This too shall pass."

I felt a wave of relief rush through me because I wanted Maya to have as normal a youth as possible and, so far, that hadn't happened. But having boy trouble certainly was in the category of normal. It made me happy.

"Thanks," I said.

He kissed my cheek. "No worries."

My dad walked ahead, and my mom came up to me and grabbed my face between her hands.

"Thank you for a wonderful dinner tonight. It's so good to be together. I'm glad you're hanging in there despite all the bad things they're saying about you everywhere."

Wow, Mom. You almost made it. You almost made it all night without mentioning it.

"Mom... I..."

She looked into my eyes. "Why would you ruin your own career like that? You were doing so well for yourself."

"Ulla! We're leaving now," my dad yelled from the doorway.

"I just don't get it, that's all," she added.

"That is absolutely no surprise to me," I said, then kissed her cheek goodbye.

NINETEEN

As he realized something was off with his toilet—the water was splashing against the sides, and there was water on the bathroom floor—Sven Thomsen forgot all about calling the police and had to call the plumber instead. Of course, the plumber arrived after dark with some excuse that it had been a busy day and he had lots of emergency calls.

Sven didn't want to hear his excuses but guided him directly to the bathroom and showed him the puddle next to the toilet.

"It's leaking."

The plumber knelt next to it and pulled out his toolbox. Sven stayed and watched the plumber to make sure he didn't mess up more than he fixed. You never knew with these types. But as he stood there, his phone suddenly rang, and he walked into the living room to answer it.

"Hi, Dad."

It was his daughter. She lived in Copenhagen with her husband and Sven's three grandchildren. Why they had to move all the way over there, he didn't understand, but just as little did he understand why they didn't come back. Fanoe island was such a good place to live. And clean. There was no reason for them to be living in that big, dirty city when they could be out here where the children could grow up running on the beach and in the forest. Sven had grown up here and enjoyed every moment of it.

It was something about a job. Jeanie, his daughter, had gotten some fancy position in the human resource department of a big software company and they had to live in Copenhagen for that. Why she was so keen on having a career and not taking care of her children was beyond Sven. He had had a career, yes, but not his wife.

"At least have one of you stay home and take care of the children," he had told her back then. "You can't both have big careers and have a family at the same time. It's not fair to the little ones."

But Jeanie had laughed at him and called him a dinosaur while patting him on the cheek in that way she did that to her seemed affectionate but to him felt condescending. Yes, Sven was getting older, and he was retired, but he wasn't old. Not really old. Sixty-seven was hardly old. At least it didn't feel like that.

"How are you doing, Dad?" Jeanie now asked, her voice soft. He could sense her exaggerated sympathy oozing all the way through the phone. Pity, he called it. This was a pity call.

"Me? I'm fine."

"Good. Good. Are you getting enough to eat?" she asked.

"Why wouldn't I eat?"

"I don't know... just since it was always... Mom who cooked..."

"So, did you assume that just because your mother died I wouldn't eat food?" he asked, trying to keep an eye on the plumber at the same time. He didn't trust him much. Still, he didn't want him to listen in on his conversation either, so he had to keep his distance. He just hoped the plumber would be able to fix the problem quickly.

"No... no, of course not..." Jeanie sighed. "Why do you have to be so... all the time... can't we just talk?"

"I don't know, Jeanie. Can you call just because you want to talk to me, not because you feel sorry for me?"

His daughter sighed again. He had hurt her. He knew he had and regretted it. He opened his mouth to say something. He wanted to express that he was, in fact, happy that she called him because he missed her and the kids terribly and he felt so alone, but his daughter beat him to it.

"I have to go, Dad. I'll call again later this week."

She hung up before he could say anything, and he put the phone down on the table next to his picture of him and Birthe. It was taken before she had received that stupid phone call from her doctor telling her it had spread.

"Stupid doctors," Sven now said to the picture. "You were fine before you went to that checkup. We were all doing fine."

Sven was a doctor himself, or he used to be, so he was allowed to call them stupid and ignorant if he wanted to. He hadn't been a physician but had worked in a lab and was very proud of his research for which he had won many prizes, which were now hanging on his wall in his study gathering dust, while the world forgot his name.

That stupid neighbor still hasn't cleared his sidewalk.

Sven grumbled and walked to the window, then peeked out when the plumber came out of the bathroom, and Sven forgot the police once again.

The plumber wiped his fingers on a towel. Sven hoped it was one he had brought himself and not one of Sven's. He wouldn't know how to get all that black stuff off it. Birthe would have known how, but it wasn't like she had left a manual on how to do things around the house when she died. There was no darn manual for anything in life.

"I... I can't really find the leak," he said.

"You can't find it?" Sven asked, annoyed. "The water was right there. On the floor. Didn't you see it? It was quite hard to miss."

"Yes, of course, but I can't find any cracks in the toilet, and it's not clogged or anything."

"Oh. Then what do you want me to do about it?" Sven asked, irritated. If he called in an expert, he expected them to get the job done, not leave without any answers.

"It might be an animal of some sort. We're getting that a lot lately; you know with the freezing temperatures we've had and all. Animals seek shelter in the pipes and then—"

"You're telling me some animal dripped water on my tiles. That it crawled out of the toilet and into my bathroom. Then let me ask you one more question. Where the heck is that animal now?"

"It could have crawled back—" the plumber tried to speak, but Sven was tired of listening to his nonsense. It was like everything else in this stupid world. If he wanted something done, he'd have to do it himself.

"Just get out of here," he told him and opened the front door.

"Call me if anything else happens or if it gets worse," the plumber said, but Sven had already slammed the door shut. He walked through the living room, grumbling about his neighbor and how he was definitely going to call the police on him first thing in the morning.

TWENTY

"You kissed Alex?"

Christina paused on the other end. Maya had returned from dinner and was sitting on her bed watching Netflix when she called. Maya's heart dropped.

"What did you say?"

"It's all over the group chat," she said. "Didn't you see it?"

"I left the group chat long ago," Maya said.

"Oh, well... but it is. Everyone is talking about you two. I knew you'd come around. I have to admit, I'm kind of jealous. He is so—"

"Yummy, I know. You said that," Maya said with a deep exhale. "Exactly who is saying that we kissed?"

"Well, he is."

"Alexander?" Maya asked.

"Yes. He said you two kissed this afternoon in front of your house... wait... it's not true?"

"Let's just say it's complicated," Maya said.

"How can it be complicated? Either you kissed or you didn't," Christina continued. "So, did you?"

"Kind of."

Christina shrieked on the other end. "I can't believe it. So, are you two like an item now? You must be; I know you, and you don't run around kissing just anyone."

"It's not like that," Maya said and closed the lid of her computer. "He kissed me. I didn't kiss him back."

Christina went quiet on the other end. "Oh."

"Yes, now you understand my reluctance to... I can't believe he's telling everyone... what the heck is he up to?"

"I guess he's proud," Christina said.

"Of what? Forcing a kiss on me... a kiss I didn't want?"

"Well, no matter what, everyone thinks you're dating now. They're totally shipping you two. You are the new hot thing."

"I don't even know the guy," Maya said, then looked out into the darkness where the snowflakes were still falling. If it kept this up all night, they'd have to close the school tomorrow. Maya secretly hoped they would. She couldn't bear the thought of having to face the entire school tomorrow. Not after this.

What kind of an idiot tells the whole school?

"So, are you going to date him at least?" Christina asked.

"Christina, we've been over this. I'm not looking for a boyfriend. I'm not remotely interested in having one."

Christina sighed. "Okay. I am a little relieved, I have to admit. I know I keep saying that he is so hot and all, and that you should date him, but the more I think about it, the more I fear losing you to him. If you two become an item, then you'll be one of the popular ones, and I'll be left all alone."

Maya chuckled. "That's not going to happen. I'm not going to date Alexander, and I am certainly not becoming one of the popular kids. There's no chance of that; don't you worry."

After that, they hung up, and Maya thought for a long time about Samuel while watching the snow dance outside her window. She had let herself fall for him and look where that got her. For all she knew, Alexander could be a serial killer. It wasn't like they carried a sign around warning people.

TWENTY-ONE

He fell asleep in his recliner as usual. Ever since Birthe had left him, he had been terrible at keeping bedtimes and instead watched TV till he couldn't hold his eyes open anymore. It was just easier that way. Then when he woke up in the middle of the night, still in his chair, he would fumble into bed and sleep the rest of the night.

It made it easier for him because he often couldn't fall asleep with no one beside him in the big bed. His daughter had recently suggested he get rid of the old king-size bed and get one that was more fitting for just one person instead.

"If you did, it would make room for a desk or a chair to sit in and read instead."

"Why would I need a desk or another chair?" he had asked her. "I have plenty of chairs. Besides, I don't like to read. Your mother liked to read. Not me."

He didn't want to give up his bed. Sven loved the bed. He had been sleeping there for thirty years with the love of his life, and now his daughter wanted to change it out, just like that. Was it really that easy for her to forget her mother? To remove any trace of her existence? Not to Sven. He wanted to keep things the way they had always been, even her clothes on her side of the wardrobe.

He dreamt about her while sleeping in the recliner, the TV muted, just as he always did. She came to him, embraced him, and everything was the way it was supposed to be. He was back at his job at the lab that he loved so much, and she was by his side at night. This time, he dreamt that they were sitting in the garden drinking lemonade on a Sunday afternoon. He was reading the paper—mostly skimming headlines—while she read her book. Some silly romance probably. Sven would say something funny about the half-naked guy on the cover, and then he would laugh, while she continued to ignore him.

Those were the times, the good times.

Sven was pulled away from his good times when a noise woke him up. He opened his eyes with a grunt only to realize everything was back to what it had been before he fell asleep. Birthe was no longer there, she wasn't reading her silly novel, and the sun wasn't shining.

But there was something else, a sound that annoyed Sven. That stupid sound of water dripping onto the bathroom floor.

"Stupid plumber who can't find a simple leak," Sven mumbled, then tried to fall back asleep. He'd have to call the guy again tomorrow; there really wasn't much else he could do right now, was there?

Maybe place some towels on the floor to minimize the damage.

Sven didn't really want to get up from his recliner. He wanted to return to that place in the sun, the one where she was still there, where the world was right again.

But the dripping sound continued and soon seemed to grow louder. Maybe it was just something he imagined; maybe it wasn't growing louder, but it just felt that way because it was so darn annoying. Fact was, he couldn't fall back asleep. He sat there in his chair, grumbling and groaning about the plumber and how incompetent he was when the dripping sound soon became something else. Now it was more of a slithering, slurping sound, one he didn't recognize. If he didn't know better, he would almost think that the water was moving.

Nonsense. It's dripping slowly onto the floor and will leave a puddle, that's all. Nothing I can't wipe up tomorrow.

Sven grumbled some more, then closed his eyes and tried to fall back asleep again. But the sound grew louder, and now it seemed it was approaching him, coming closer and closer. The slurping and slithering noises reached his chair, then stopped right behind him.

Heart in his throat, Sven shot his eyes open, then sat up straight just in time to look into the creature's eyes before it forced waves of liquid inside his body. Sven gurgled and fought to breathe while wondering if Birthe would be where he was going after this.

He doubted it.

TWENTY-TWO

I opened my eyes with a gasp and stared at the ceiling. I had been dreaming about Victor. In my dream, Victor had disappeared, and I couldn't find him anywhere. Every time I thought I saw him and reached out for him, he would run away from me, holding Skye's hand. I could still hear Skye's giggling as she pulled my son away from me.

The dream left me feeling awful about myself. It didn't take a dream expert to analyze it, and it made me feel like the worst mother in the world. It wasn't like Skye had ever giggled like that or was even a mean person. I knew she wasn't. She was just a very good friend to Victor and one who had finally made him happy.

Why was I acting like this?

I lay still for a little while, willing away the sensation that the dream had left me with. While I lay there, staring into the darkness, I thought I heard something. It sounded like the pipes in my house. They were creaking and almost moaning.

It had to be freezing out. Usually, the pipes would be very noisy when they froze over. I just prayed they wouldn't crack.

I can't remember them being this noisy, though.

I sat up in my bed, slightly worried. The noise grew into loud banging sounds, and I wondered if it had anything to do with what I had experienced earlier in the downstairs bathroom.

Is it frogs? Please, let it just be frogs.

The noise stopped just as abruptly as it had started, and I fell back in the bed with a deep sigh, my head sinking into the pillow. I closed my eyes to go back to sleep, but thoughts of my book and the newspapers and my publisher rummaged in my mind and wouldn't let me rest.

Had I really made a mistake like they all said? Had I destroyed my career? I was beginning to think so.

No, I love this book. I should stand up for myself. They'll come around. They'll see. Just give it time.

I managed to doze off, but a sound woke me up again. It wasn't the same as earlier; this one was different. It sounded like it was raining... inside.

DRIP-DRIP-DRIP.

My eyes shot open, and I looked around me. The sound was coming from my bathroom. The door was ajar, and light was coming out from behind it. I had forgotten to shut it off. The dripping was followed by a slithering sound, like something big was moving across the floor, something big and wet. The slithering sound soon became more of a slushing one, almost slurping, and I found myself staring at the door and the small crack of light, my heart pounding in my chest.

Something was in there, something wet and slimy.

Was it a snake?

I shuddered at the thought, then got out of my bed. As I put on my slippers, I spotted Brutus. He was sitting in my room, also staring at the bathroom door. I looked at the door to my bedroom. It was slightly ajar, and he had to have snuck in here during the night.

"Gosh, you scared me, Brutus," I said and held my chest.

I stared at the dog with the shining eyes, then wondered how he had gotten out of Victor's room where he usually slept with Victor and Skye. I distinctly remembered having left him there with them, sitting in the corner, watching them the way he always did. I had wondered—like so many times before—if the dog even slept at all. He seemed to be awake twenty-four seven, always watching Victor.

As I approached him, I could hear him growling. A low deep growl that sounded almost like a rumble. Brutus never made a sound, so that coming from him was quite alarming to me. Something was definitely in that bathroom. Something that had Brutus on his toes.

"You hear it too, huh, buddy?" I said to him and stood beside him while the slithering and slurping noises continued in my bathroom.

I wondered if I was going to find a python in there. It had to be that size to make a sound like that.

"Never met a frog that made a sound like that," I said.

I wondered for a second if I should just close the door and call the plumber—or maybe an exterminator—in the morning, but my curiosity got the better of me. If that thing came through my pipes, it could get anywhere in the house. I had to know at least what I was dealing with here.

"Okay, Brutus, I'm going in. I expect you to have my back, all right?" I said to the dog. His low rumbling made me believe he agreed. If anyone ever had my back, I knew it would be him. Somehow, I just knew. Maybe because he had saved me once before.

I walked to the door and grabbed the handle with a deep inhale, bracing myself for what might wait behind it. I pulled it fully open. As I did, whatever it was that was lurking in there moved fast and disappeared down the drain of my bathtub. I hurried inside just in time to see it slip through the small holes, looking like water being sucked down fast.

What the heck?

I realized I was standing in a puddle of water and groaned. There had to be a leak somewhere.

Or maybe the animal dripped onto the floor, leaving the puddle.

But that made no sense. No big animal could come out of that tiny drain and get back in that fast. But no small animal could have made that big of a puddle or that loud of a sound either.

I didn't get it. It made no sense.

"Maybe I was still dreaming, huh?" I asked Brutus who had come to the door and was sitting in the opening. He had stopped growling.

"Nah, it was probably just a frog," I said and turned off the lights before I walked back toward my bed, Brutus following me closely. I let him stay in my room the rest of the night in the hope he would warn and protect me should this creature—that I still hoped and prayed was nothing but a frog—decide to return.

TWENTY-THREE

"Sounds like you have rats," Sophia said. "I had rats once in the attic, and they made an awful noise at night."

I sat down and placed a cup of coffee in front of her. I hadn't slept much more that night and felt exhausted. Both Victor and Maya had left for school, and Skye was in Victor's room as usual when he wasn't here, waiting for him to come back. I was beginning to wonder what to do about the girl. She needed to go to school soon and not just hang out around here, but I didn't know how to have her go without alerting the authorities. For some reason, I didn't dare to.

Morten was my ally in this, and he was doing what he could to search for her parents and keep an eye out for anyone looking for a child her age, but so far, he hadn't found any matches. The problem was, I couldn't really let them take her away. Not just because it would devastate Victor. It most certainly would. But I also feared for what they might do to her if she became a number in the system or if anyone discovered what she was capable of. I just couldn't figure out where she had come from and why no one seemed to miss her.

"You really think it could be rats?" I asked. "I mean, there was a big puddle on the floor, and just how would a rat get through my drain? The holes aren't very big. They're like the size of a small coin."

"Rats have been known to get in and out of places that seemed impossible before. That wouldn't stop them. Ugh. I hate those creatures. So nasty and hard to get rid of, might I add."

I sipped my coffee, shuddering. "I hate rats."

"You probably need to get an exterminator out here to have a look at it," Sophia said and grabbed a piece of mint chocolate that I had put out on the table for us. My laptop was lying next to me, the lid still closed. It was getting harder and harder to resist it. A big part of me desperately wanted to go online and check what the reviewers said or check out my social media, but Sophia had told me it was still too early. She was here to keep me company, so I wouldn't fall in, she had told me when she walked into my kitchen this morning and asked for coffee, ASAP.

"Besides it's a lot more fun to hang out here than clean the house after six kids ate breakfast," she added.

I, for one, was grateful for her visits. Especially today when I didn't like being alone in this big house. I felt the entire house was creaking and moaning with the cold north wind blowing outside. After the night I had, I didn't feel comfortable being here.

"Say, have you ever heard about a plumber who disappeared back in the eighties?" I asked.

Sophia looked at me, then shook her head. "Not that I can recall. I was just a young child back then. Why?"

I shrugged. "The plumber who was here yesterday told me he had a colleague who disappeared at Fishy Pines back then. I've been thinking about that all night while lying awake."

"Why? Couldn't the guy have just disappeared because he wanted to? Maybe because he was tired of working where everyone poops. Maybe because he was sick of his wife and the life he was living. It's happened before. Someone telling their wife they're going for cigarettes and then never coming back. He's probably sitting on some Caribbean island by now."

"I have a problem with that assumption. Why do people keep saying that? What if something happened to him?"

"Then we would have found his body by now, don't you think? No body, no crime, right?" Sophia said.

"Maybe, maybe not," I said and sipped my coffee.

Sophia observed me. "Ah, I get it. You see a story there, don't you? You want to write a new book."

I shrugged and grabbed another chocolate. "I don't know if there's anything there yet, but I just have this feeling that I need to look into it."

TWENTY-FOUR

It had to be the most embarrassing day of her life. Maya walked the hallways of school, her backpack slung over her shoulder, while everyone—nearly everyone—she passed smiled and nodded at her, looking like they shared some deep secret. Some of the girls were pointing fingers at her while whispering to one another as she walked past them.

"Why are they doing that?" Maya asked Christina while fighting her blushing red cheeks.

"They're impressed with you," she said.

"Impressed? What is there to be impressed with?" Maya asked, surprised and a little annoyed.

"Uh, duh. Alexander kissed you. He's only the number one most popular guy in the school, and he doesn't walk around kissing just anyone. As a matter of fact, you're the first who anyone has heard of. Many a girl has tried to get him to kiss her, but without luck."

Maya scoffed. "It's really not that impressive. I wish they would all just leave me alone."

They walked into the classroom for history. Alex was sitting in his seat, surrounded by his friends. They looked at him with admiration as he spoke.

The entire classroom went silent when Maya entered, and all eyes were on the two of them. Someone gasped while most of the others held their breath. Maya felt like they were the most ridiculous people in the world.

"Hey, Maya," Alex said and gave her one of his famous smiles. Now, all eyes were on her. Would she respond back?

She did, but not in a way that Alex had expected. Maya simply groaned loudly, then sat down at her own desk and pulled out her books. Whispers filled the room, and soon Alex was losing face.

"Wow," Christina said and sat next to her. "That was brutal. You totally destroyed him there."

"Well, he deserves it," Maya said. "For thinking he can tell lies about me and then expect me to be nice to him."

But Alex wasn't going to give up just like that. With the entire class following his every move, he walked to her desk and sat on it.

"I like your shirt," he said. "It really brings out your eyes."

Maya looked up at him, then shook her head. "Where do you get your lines from? A book or the internet?"

He laughed like she had said something funny and shook his head like they were enjoying each other's company. The teacher then walked in, and Alex leaned over and whispered in Maya's ear, "I will get you to change your mind. Just you wait and see."

Maya answered with another groan, but as she was about to say something, the teacher started class and Alex rushed to his seat. During the entire class, he kept looking at her, sending her air kisses, and winking at her every time she accidentally looked his way.

What was his deal? Why was he so insistent on having her? Was it just because he couldn't? Because he could have any other girl in school except her? Maybe. But Maya didn't want to be a part of his games. She wanted to be left alone. She had burned her fingers on a boy before and wasn't going to be so stupid as to do it again. This guy had all the traits of a true psychopath, and she wasn't falling for that again.

TWENTY-FIVE

"John Andersen disappeared on January 25, 1982. His wife was expecting him home for dinner, but he never made it. His boss told the police that he responded to a job at Fishy Pines right before the end of the day. That's the last anyone ever heard of him."

I looked at Morten while reading from the police report. I had been researching all day since Sophia left me, without even checking my social media or googling my name even once—an accomplishment I was very proud of. Now it was late afternoon, and Morten had stopped by. Maya was in her room as usual, while Victor and Skye played in the garden.

"His wife told the police that she was waiting at home with pork chops and mashed potatoes, his favorite dishes, and she knew he would never stay away from that on purpose. He had promised her he would be home at six and so she counted on it. When he didn't arrive, she thought he had been held up at work; that happened often. 'But he would always come home. Never more than half an hour late,' she said.

"So as the clock struck ten, she called the police, who came out and talked to her. They calmed her down and told her to wait and see if he didn't show up eventually, but after two days, they started their search of the island. With no results. The guy had vanished. Listen to what she added here. 'I could have understood it if I had served chicken or a salad or something, but John would never stay away from my pork chops. Not my John.'"

I looked at Morten with a wry smile. He shrugged and drank his coffee. "So what? It's thirty-six years ago. People disappear from time to time, most of them do so deliberately. You know, running from debt or from a life they can't stand anymore."

"Or... maybe something happened to him," I said.

Morten scoffed. He glared at me. "Say, exactly where did you get all that information?"

I pushed the police report that I had printed aside. "Newspapers and stuff."

He shook his head. "I don't believe you. Did you hack into the police server again? Are you just looking for trouble?"

I sighed. "The newspapers didn't exactly write much about it. They printed his picture and wrote that he was missing, but they didn't report much else. No details. I needed details. For my book."

He sipped his coffee and gave me a look. "I can't continue looking away, you know... when you keep doing stupid stuff."

"I really think there might be a story here," I said, ignoring his threats.

"How so? You have no body, no crime, no witnesses," he said.

"Actually, there was one. Witness." I pulled out a piece of paper from the report. "I had to go deep into the files to find her, but there was one woman who was there when he arrived at Fishy Pines. She was the nurse on duty, and she let him in."

"And what did she say?"

"That's the strange thing. Her name is here, see, but there is no statement. Not according to the records. I can't find it anywhere."

"It may not be there digitally. Maybe it's in the old files in the basement of the station," he said and put his cup down.

I leaned forward and looked into his eyes. "And that's where you come in."

"No, no, no, Emma. I don't have time for this... I am—"

"I know you don't want to be involved but come on. It's one little trip to the basement. Just look for her statement, and you'll make me a very happy gal."

Morten looked at me with an exhale. I leaned over and kissed him, then looked into his eyes.

"Pretty please?"

He sighed. "All right. All right. Now I have to get home. I promised Jytte I'd have dinner with her tonight and binge watch *Stranger Things*."

I made a disappointed sound. "I thought we were having dinner."

"Please, don't start, Emma. It doesn't matter what I do; I always end up disappointing someone," he said. "Between you and Jytte, I can't win."

"All right," I said.

Morten leaned down and kissed me again.

"Tomorrow then?"

"I'll stop by at some point during the day. I promised Jytte I would take her to see a film at night. I can do dinner with you first."

I sighed, disappointed again. I couldn't really be mad at him for wanting to be with his child, but the girl was nineteen and done with school. How long was she planning on still living at home? She had a job now; she could easily pay for some small condo downtown. It was like she was clinging to her father lately. Maybe because she knew that, as soon as she left, he would probably move in with me.

Why do I think like that? The poor girl simply loves her father and wants to be with him.

"All right," I said and blew him another kiss. "But you gotta promise me to spend the night soon. I miss being close to you. I mean dinners and coffee are nice and all, but we need more than that."

He nodded, then touched my cheek gently. "I know. And we will. It's just that between you and her, I feel kind of worn out. Plus, Jytte doesn't like me staying away at night. Makes her feel lonely, she says."

"She should get a boyfriend," I said.

"Yeah, well, I'm in no rush with that part. Right now, it seems she's very vulnerable. Since she finished school, she's been very isolated and keeping to herself at my house, almost hiding out, only leaving to go to work, a job I found for her because she was just lying there at home on the couch or in her bed doing nothing."

"What about college?"

He sighed. It was the worried kind. "I don't know what to tell you, Emma. It's like she doesn't want to. I keep telling her to apply so she can start after the summer, but she doesn't even want to talk about it. I think the future frightens her because all of her friends know what they want to do, but she doesn't."

"I am sorry, Morten. I didn't know."

He nodded, smiling. "It's okay. She just needs a little extra attention from me these days, till she pushes through this. Just bear with me, will you?"

I nodded. "Of course. Our kids come before anything else, right?"

He kissed me again, then rushed out the door while I stared at the police report in front of me and glared at the name of the nurse.

"Laila Lund. Where are you now, Laila Lund?"

TWENTY-SIX

He loathed shoveling snow. Christian Staun had woken up at five o'clock this morning to clear off the sidewalk. Why? Because his grumpy old neighbor had threatened to call the police on him if he didn't do it. It was the law, yes, but Christian didn't exactly have much time to uphold it. Between running his own refrigerator business and taking care of his paralyzed wife all on his own, there really weren't many available hours in the day. Besides, it kept snowing, so it didn't really matter if he cleared the sidewalk in front of his house or not. It would only be covered again in those traitorous whirling flakes within the next hour, and he'd have to start all over.

But the law was the law. Especially according to his nosy and bitter neighbor. So, this morning, Christian had finally taken up the fight with the white mass. Just to please his old neighbor. And his wife. Mostly his wife, who wanted him to keep in good standing with the neighbors.

It was all his fault that she ended up the way she had. They had been at a business dinner, one of those where Christian knew if he gave it all he had, he would land the client. And he had. He had landed the greatest and most lucrative deal of his life, one that would mean millions and change their lives forever.

They told him there was nothing he could have done differently to avoid the lorry. It came out of nowhere, the police said. So fast he wouldn't have been able to react even if he had superpowers. But Christian was the one who had turned his head to yell at his son in the back seat. Christian didn't even remember why he had yelled at the boy, no matter how many times he went through the event in his mind; he simply couldn't recall why it was or what he had said.

He only knew it had been the last thing he had ever said to the boy. And it hadn't been nice.

His wife, Brigitte, had told him to let it go. To stop obsessing about it, but he still did. He wanted to know why he had yelled; he wanted to justify his actions... he wanted it to matter. Otherwise, it was just too unbearable. Unforgivable. He turned his head away, took his eyes off the road ahead. An action that cost his wife the ability to move anything from the waist down and the precious life of his dear son.

Christian threw a shovelful of snow onto the pile in the garden. He grunted and complained while more snowflakes danced around his head and got thicker and thicker.

"Great. More snow," he sighed, annoyed. This entire sidewalk, the area he had cleaned off, would be covered again by the time the sun rose.

He stared at it, then looked at his neighbor's house. By the time the old man woke up, the snow would have covered it all again, and Christian would be at work. The old geezer wouldn't even see what he had done, would he? Of course not.

I'll make him, dang it. I'll make him if I have to.

Christian threw the shovel on the pile of snow, then walked with angry steps up the neighbor's driveway, then placed a finger on his doorbell. He knew the old man was probably still asleep, but Christian didn't care. The geezer was going to see what he had done if it was the last thing he ever did.

When no one opened the door, Christian took to knocking. He knocked harder and harder.

"SVEN!" he yelled while hammering on the door. "Come out here and see what I've done. I want you to come out here, dang it!"

Christian panted, agitated and angry, as he kept pounding on the door. The old man was going to see this whether he liked it or not. No matter the hour.

Finally, Christian grabbed the handle and turned it and, much to his surprise, the door opened.

"SVEN," Christian yelled. "Come out here!"

Thinking he'd have to go into his bedroom and wake the old man, Christian walked into the living room, then stopped. He didn't have to walk any farther. The old man was sitting right there in his recliner.

"Sven?"

Christian knew before he even approached him. He had seen a dead person up close before. He had found his own dad after he had killed himself back when Christian was eleven and came home from school. Not that Sven looked anything like his dad, who had hung himself. But they had one thing in common —no, make that two—the smell and the flies.

TWENTY-SEVEN

I woke up early because so much was on my mind, and I decided to walk the dogs before everyone else woke up and all the chaos that was called my life erupted. The snow had picked up again, so I decided to walk on the street instead of on the beach. I liked the quietness of the mornings, and the thick snow made it so quaint. I also enjoyed the fact that I was awake before most people.

I continued out of my neighborhood and across the street into another neighborhood. Brutus followed closely behind me as always, while I kept Kenneth Two on a tight leash as he was known to run into people's gardens and bark at some squirrel or bird or someone's rubbish bin (yes, it happened before). Kenneth was pulling me forcefully ahead, tugging so hard on the leash that he almost ran out of breath.

"Easy there," I said to him. "You're gonna choke yourself."

He did his business in someone's driveway, and I hurried to remove it before anyone saw it, then rushed ahead.

I walked past a house, then stopped at the sidewalk and stared. It was completely cleared from snow. Who in their right mind had been shoveling snow at this hour?

Kenneth pulled me past it and into the neighbor's driveway. The door opened, and someone ran out. This person was not looking where he was going and slammed into me so hard that I fell backward into a pile of snow.

"Hey!"

Kenneth took to barking at the guy, then attacked the man's boot and bit into it while growling like he was trying to rip it off him.

"Hey, get your stupid dog off me," the guy yelled.

I managed to get up from the ground and brushed the snow off my clothes. The man grumbled at Kenneth and tried to kick him. I grabbed Kenneth and pulled at him, but the crazy dog wouldn't let go, no matter how much I scolded him.

"Kenneth! Dang it, let go!"

I had to stick my fingers inside the dog's mouth, like I did when he had accidentally eaten something he wasn't supposed to on the beach and I had to pull it out. I forced his jaws to open and, finally, he let go. I held the growling and barking dog in my arms as the man looked at his boot.

"Great. Now it's completely ruined. They're supposed to keep water out and now... look at those holes."

"Hey, mister. You're the one who stormed outside without even looking where you were going. The dog only tried to protect me."

I couldn't believe I was actually making excuses for Kenneth. There really was a first time for everything, wasn't there?

"Yeah? Well... well... you were... period."

"What?" He was making no sense. That was when I realized the man was paler than the snow surrounding us. "Are you all right?"

He looked into my eyes. "You know what? No, I'm not. I really am not. I just found... my neighbor..." the man pointed at the door he had left open.

"Did something happen to your neighbor?" I asked, trying to make sense of what he was saying.

"He's... I found him... I was just going in there because he is always, *always,* on my case about the snow shoveling and I wanted him to see it... I just wanted to make sure... it was all in vain..."

I didn't want to wait for the guy to make any sense, so instead, I walked up the driveway and into the house. I spotted the man in the recliner, then walked up to him. The man from the street followed me and came up behind me.

"What do you think happened to him? I mean, he was old and all," he said. "Do you think he just had a heart attack?"

I sighed, then shrugged. "I don't know. Let me call the police."

I put Kenneth down, then grabbed my phone. As I called Morten's number, I realized I was standing in a puddle of water. Waiting for him to pick up, I reached down and touched it. It seemed to be water, it even looked like water, but it felt a little thicker, and it had a slight smell to it. One I recognized from my own bathroom.

TWENTY-EIGHT

Maya woke up when something hit her window. She sat up, feeling slightly woozy as her dream left her body and she returned to reality. What was that? A bird?

She walked to the window and looked out when something else hit the window. It was a snowball. It left a lump of snow that slid down the glass. Baffled, Maya looked down in her garden where she spotted Alexander.

What the heck?

She opened the window and shuddered as the icy breeze hit her face.

"Maya," he said.

"What are you doing here? What time is it?" she asked and looked at the clock by her TV with a light gasp. She had overslept.

"I wanted to walk to school with you," he said. "But you didn't open your front door when I rang the bell."

"Shoot. I'm late. I didn't wake up. My mom usually wakes me up!"

"Well, get ready fast, and we'll walk to school together."

Maya closed the window as quickly as she could and

grabbed her phone. Her mom had called seven times. She had left a voicemail, and Maya listened to it while finding her clothes. Her mother babbled something about her having to stay somewhere where they found a dead body. They had to wait for the police to arrive, so Maya would have to get herself and Victor ready for school. Maya sighed. So typical of her mother. Now she had to take care of herself *and* Victor.

Maya ran into the hallway. She peeked inside Victor's room. Victor and Skye were already awake. They were sitting on the carpet, both in the lotus position, floating just a few centimeters above the ground, eyes closed and holding hands.

Maya shook her head. She had no time for this.

"Victor!"

He fell to the floor.

"Your bus is coming in a few minutes," Maya said. "Get ready!"

Maya didn't wait to see if he heard what she had said. She went to the bathroom and took the fastest shower she had ever taken, then got dressed and ran downstairs and grabbed a banana, just as the Fishy Pines bus drove up.

"Victor! The bus is here!"

Victor came down with his backpack on his back. Maya handed him a banana as he walked out, not wearing any shoes. Maya didn't realize he was only in his socks till he had gotten on the bus. She ran outside with his shoes in her hand, but the bus had already departed. As she turned around to go back in, she spotted Alexander.

"Rough morning, huh?"

"Oh, dear. I completely forgot about you. Have you been out here all this time? You must be freezing!"

He shrugged. His nose was red, and he had snow on his eyebrows. Maya was filled with a deep embarrassment. Maybe she had been too tough on the guy.

"Come on in," she said. "I'll make you some tea."

"Really? I'd love to, but we'll be late for school."

"We will be anyway," Maya said. "I think we can skip the first class of the day without anyone noticing us. We'll blame it on the snow, how about that? What do you say?"

Alexander's face lit up. "I say I'd like a little milk in my tea, please."

TWENTY-NINE

"How do you constantly manage to get yourself involved in these types of things?" Morten asked.

I shrugged. "I was just walking the dog."

He shook his head with a chuckle. "You are something, Emma. You truly are."

He had come about fifteen minutes after I called him. He had been asleep, and it took a little while for him to understand exactly what I was telling him. Now we were sitting in the dead man's living room, staring at him while waiting for Dr. Williamsen to arrive. Dr. Williamsen was an old man, and the island's only doctor, but he didn't move fast. Not that there was any reason to rush. The man was dead, no doubt about it.

Christian Staun, the man who had bumped into me, was there too, and Morten had taken his statement. I was slightly worried about his condition because he kept mumbling weird things. I feared he might lose it, so I had told Morten it might be a good idea for Dr. Williamsen to have a little chat with him before he rushed off to work as was his intention.

"I think he's about to explode, but I could be wrong," I said.

After talking to him, Morten had agreed. The man couldn't

be sent off to work like that. He hadn't stayed with us all the time because he had a wife at his house that he cared for, so he had gone back there and made sure she had something to eat before he returned.

"So, how do you think he died?" I asked and looked at Sven Thomsen, as I had learned the dead man's name was, or had been.

"Looks like old age, maybe a heart attack," he said.

"Will you have him autopsied?" I asked.

Morten shook his head. "Depends on what Dr. Williamsen says, but I hardly see any reason to. He was old."

"In his sixties. That's hardly old, I argued.

"True," Morten said. "It could have been his heart. Maybe the doctor will know."

I gave him a look, and he sighed. "No, Emma, I don't think it has anything to do with what happened to Ann Mortensen."

"You had her autopsied. Why not this guy?"

"It was her husband who requested it," he said. "I agreed because I thought it might give him peace of mind to know how she died."

"You think he killed her?" I asked. "Her husband? You think he drowned her, then pulled her back to her bed to make it look like she just died in her sleep?"

"And then requested an autopsy? Kind of sounds like a weird way to try to get away with murder, but I know that the detectives from the mainland who are looking into it have had him in for questioning. It just doesn't really make sense."

"True." I looked at the puddle on the floor. Morten saw me do it.

"I know what you're thinking," he said.

"Were Ann Mortensen's clothes wet?" I asked.

"Yes," he said.

I felt Sven Thomsen's shirt. "Same here. It's black so you

can't see it, but it's soaked. And there's water on the floor right next to him. Just like at Ann Mortensen's house."

Morten sighed. "I don't even want to know how you know that, but please leave the police work to the professionals, okay?"

I forced a smile. "Okay."

THIRTY

They forgot the time. Maya and Alexander stayed in Maya's kitchen for hours while talking and completely forgot to go to school. Maya sipped her tea while listening to Alex tell her about his family and his younger brother who took up so much of his parents' time, no one ever looked at what Alex did.

That was when it occurred to Maya that she had misjudged Alex from the beginning. He wasn't shallow. He wasn't just a pretty face. He was actually pleasant to be with and amazing to talk to. She had never talked to a guy and felt so comfortable before. Not with Samuel, not even with Asgar, who had been her close friend.

"More tea?" she asked.

Alexander nodded and gave her his cup. As he did, their fingertips brushed, and Maya blushed. She turned away.

"I... I think... do you want some milk in that?"

He smiled and nodded. "Yes, please."

She served him another cup, then sat down, her eyes avoiding his. She had promised herself never to fall for this guy, but it was getting increasingly harder not to. His glance caught hers and held on to it. It made her stomach burst with butterflies.

Oh, girl. I'm in trouble now!

"I'm really enjoying this," he said. "Us two here. Talking like this." He sighed and leaned forward.

Maya exhaled.

"I want to know everything about you, Maya," he said with a low raspy voice. "I want to know all about your family. Who are you? Who is Maya Frost?"

Maya stared into his eyes while contemplating what to do or say next. His soft eyes were piercing hers, and she felt her hands get clammy.

Say something!

But she couldn't. She didn't dare to tell him about herself. So far, they had talked about him and his family, and he had told stories of their holidays in Italy and his soccer team and how he was awarded player of the year last year, but she had told him nothing. How could she? How could she tell him about her brother and his strange friend? Her family was so weird while Alex's was so typical.

He can never know.

Fearing he would end up telling people at the school or just plain laughing at her, she decided to play it safe.

"There really isn't much to tell. We're pretty boring really."

"Well, your mom isn't exactly boring," he said. "She's pretty cool if you ask me."

"The media doesn't seem to think so lately," Maya said.

She had seen the social media posts and even read some of the articles in the newspapers that people shared, but she had decided never to tell her mother. It would only crush her. She didn't need to know.

"What are you talking about? What she did only makes her even cooler, if you ask me."

Maya smiled. Alex grabbed her hand in his. "I don't think you're boring, Maya Frost. Not even a little bit."

Then he leaned across the table, almost knocking his teacup over, closing his eyes, his lips pursed. Maya sucked air in through her teeth, then closed her eyes too and let him. In the second his lips were supposed to hit hers, she heard the front door slam shut, followed by her mother's voice, yelling, "What the heck is going on here?"

THIRTY-ONE

"Why aren't you in school?"

I placed both my hands on my hips as the two teenagers stared at me, eyes wide, cheeks blushing. There was no doubt I had walked in at the exact right moment.

"Maya?" I asked.

"I... we... we..."

"It's my fault, Mrs. Frost," the boy said. I knew I had seen him before, but I didn't know his name.

"And who might you be?" I asked.

The boy rose to his feet and approached me. I don't think his face could have been redder had he just gotten out of a hot sauna. He reached out his hand.

"I'm Alexander, Mrs. Frost."

"It's Miss Frost," I said. "I'm divorced."

"Sorry, Miss Frost."

"So, it's your fault, huh? Care to explain?" I asked.

The two teenagers exchanged a look. Alexander rubbed his hands together. "I came to walk Maya to school and then... well, she had overslept and—"

"You overslept? Maya!" I said.

She rose to her feet. "Hey, I made sure Victor got to school."

"Without his shoes! They called from the school and said he arrived with soaked socks. How could you send him to school with no shoes?" I asked.

Maya scoffed. "Well, maybe if he wasn't so stupid as to walk outside without them. He's twelve, Mom. He should be able to remember his own darn shoes. I didn't realize it till the bus had left. It wasn't my fault, Mom."

I took a few deep breaths to calm myself down. I didn't succeed. I couldn't believe how careless my daughter suddenly was.

"I can't believe you. I'm not here for a few hours, and everything falls apart. You didn't even make it out the door. What were you thinking?"

Maya stared at me and crossed her arms in front of her chest with a groan. "I'm not going to listen to this," she said, grabbed her backpack, and looked at Alexander. "Come on. We have to get to school."

"Oh, now you wanna go to school, huh?" I yelled after them. "Tell me what would have happened if I hadn't walked in at this moment, huh?"

I didn't expect an answer, and I didn't get one. They had both rushed out the door and slammed it behind them. I sighed profoundly, then sat down in one of the kitchen chairs, rubbing my forehead. I grabbed one of the biscuits the teenagers had brought out but not even touched.

Probably busy with all the kissing, I thought. Instead of going to school, hah. I can't believe she would do that.

I didn't mind Maya having a boyfriend; she was, after all, seventeen. No, that wasn't why I was upset. I was angry because she let it affect her school and because she hadn't told me anything about this boy before. I didn't even know his name, and here they were... kissing. In my kitchen I thought she told me everything, and now this. A strange boy all over my daughter. In my own house.

I shook my head and put my feet up on the chair next to me, while Kenneth attacked a stuffed animal that Sophia's youngest, Alma, had left the last time she was here. I stared at the dog for a little while, not bothering to scold him again until my phone rang. I picked it up once I saw Morten's name on my display.

"Hey. You miss me already?"

"Ha-ha, very funny. I am actually pretty stressed out right now. I'm trying to get ahold of Sven Thomsen's family in Copenhagen to tell them the bad news. But I did have time to check out the thing you asked me to yesterday."

I sat up straight. "The statement?"

"Yes, there isn't one. They never questioned Laila Lund, according to the report."

"Why not?" I asked, reaching out for another biscuit. I was careful not to crunch loudly, so Morten wouldn't hear it. There was no reason for him to know I was eating biscuits.

"Well, apparently, she made no sense. The day after John Andersen's disappearance, she was admitted to Fishy Pines by her family. For treatment in the very institution where she worked. When they closed the adult department shortly after because the building was falling apart, she was transferred to Lakeview Mental Hospital in Sønderho. She might still be there."

THIRTY-TWO

Hanne Carlsen yawned for the third time in a row. Her coworker turned to look at her with a smile.

"Too much partying?" he asked.

"Very funny," Hanne said and grabbed the report her coworker handed her, then walked back to her computer and sat down. She punched in the numbers, then felt another yawn come along and caved into it. She stared at the flickering computer screen, her eyelids feeling heavier than ever.

She sipped from the coffee cup that stood next to her and realized it was her fourth today. She'd have to cut back soon, but she was just so darn tired all the time.

All because of that stupid leak.

It had kept her awake two nights in a row. The dripping in her bathroom. She had thought it was just the tap and tried to tighten it better the night before, but still the dripping returned last night. This morning, she had called a plumber, and her husband had stayed home to let him in. Hopefully, they would find out what it was, so she would get a better night's sleep tonight.

If only the plumber can find the leak.

Hanne hadn't been able to figure out exactly where the leak was. But a leak there was; she had no doubt in her mind. She could hear it, and she had even found a puddle of water on the bathroom floor in the morning. Her husband, Per, kept telling her she was crazy because every time she convinced him to go look for it, there was no dripping sound. He had never heard it. Still, Hanne knew it was there.

"Can you give me the results from last week's tests?" Hanne asked a coworker sitting behind her.

He handed the file to her.

"Thanks."

She opened the folder and looked at the numbers, then rubbed her forehead. "We're really making progress on this one," she said.

"Sure are," the coworker said from behind her.

Hanne smiled and sipped her coffee, hoping for the caffeine to kick in soon. Being tired and not fully alert wasn't good in her line of work.

"Any news of subject B-3?" she asked.

The coworker shook his head. "Nope."

"Dang it. I can't believe we actually lost a subject. That was years of hard work."

"I know," he said. "My guess is there will be more heads rolling soon."

"As there should be." They had fired only one after it happened, but several others were just as responsible, in her opinion.

Hanne grabbed the folder from the cabinet of subject B-3 and looked through it. The pictures of the girl levitating aboveground had been taken right before she ran away. Corporate had decided to tone the disappearance down and not report it to the police. They didn't want any media attention and had to find the subject on their own was the message. Hanne didn't know how the search was going, but she knew they were out there looking for her, going through the entire island. She pitied the fools standing in their way. These guys were no joke.

Finishing her coffee, Hanne felt the urge to rush to the bathroom, which wasn't so strange after four cups of coffee. She left the file on her desk, then hurried to the restroom, went inside a stall, and closed the door. She yawned a few times more while sitting in there and while thinking about the girl they had lost. She had been testing her for years and had come really far in cracking her genetic code, and then, just like that—puff—she was gone.

Those who were responsible deserve to get fired over this, she thought. *You don't just lose a subject worth millions in research. Tsk.*

Hanne drew in a deep breath when a noise coming from outside her stall made her freeze.

It was the sound of water leaking.

THIRTY-THREE

She was still there. The nice personnel at Lakeview Mental Hospital told me over the phone that Laila Lund had been a patient there since nineteen eighty-two and very rarely had visitors, and if I would like to come and see her, it would be very much appreciated.

So, I did. I drove to the southern part of the island, to Sønderho and parked the car outside in the parking lot. It was a gorgeous old building from the year eighteen ten that housed the hospital.

"Used to be a hotel," the nurse who showed me to Laila Lund's room explained. "One of the most beautiful and popular in the country, as a matter of fact. But then the owner died, and the state bought it to house patients. We believe the nice surroundings are good for them. Therapeutic. The garden grows to be stunning in the spring. You should come out and see it."

"Well, maybe I will," I said as we reached a door and the nurse stopped. She sighed and looked at me.

"Mrs. Lund doesn't make much sense. You'll have to bear with her, all right?"

"Of course. What happened to her?" I asked. "Do you know?"

She shook her head. "Not really. Someone once mentioned that she had a shock of some sort. That triggered it. You know, a trauma of sorts. But she has never been able to tell anyone exactly what it was."

"I see," I said.

The nurse knocked on the door and opened it. "Hi there, Mrs. Lund," she said, her voice almost singing. "You have a visitor today. A famous one. The great author Emma Frost is here to see you; maybe she'll sign a book for you before she leaves, huh?"

I blushed slightly. "Sure."

"Awesome. I'll leave you two to it then," the nurse said with a big smile, then left.

Laila Lund was sitting in a wheelchair looking out the window, her back turned to me. I approached her.

"Hi there. As the nurse said, my name is Emma Frost. And I'm here because I'm writing a book about... well, I don't really know what it's about yet, but a part of it is about the disappearance of a plumber..."

I looked down at Laila Lund, who wasn't looking out the window as I had assumed, but instead sat in her chair, staring emptily into the air, a smile plastered on her face, giggling like someone had said something funny. Drool was running out of the side of her mouth. I sighed and grabbed a chair, then sat down. I wasn't quite sure what I expected to find here. I just knew I needed answers.

"So, Laila," I said. "Can you tell me anything about John Andersen and what happened to him? I think you might have been the last person ever to see him."

I turned my head and looked at the woman to see if I would get any reaction from mentioning the man's name, but nothing came. She just sat there, grinning. I exhaled, found a napkin, and wiped off the drool from her face, then sat back down.

"The thing is," I said and looked out the window. "I think something horrible happened to him on that night when he disappeared. And I think you saw it. I also think the shock of what happened made you how you are today. So, if only there was a way to have you tell me exactly what it was you saw on that night. If only. Then maybe we could get to the bottom of this. I think there's a heck of a story to tell. But I can't seem to crack it open. I had hoped you could help."

THIRTY-FOUR

The snow-covered landscape outside Laila Lund's window had me mesmerized. I sat in the chair for about an hour or so, talking to the old woman in her chair, telling her everything I knew about the story so far and even what had happened to me earlier in the year. I don't know why I did it, but I just needed it, I guess.

Somehow, I felt that she, of all people, would understand it, or at least wouldn't tell me I was awful for thinking I had actually fought a guy who was centuries old, who drank the blood of certain people living here because it—for reasons I had yet to figure out—contained some strange green stuff that he needed in order to survive.

"I don't get it. I mean, why would Victor's blood be green? And why is he so close to Skye, closer than he has ever been to me?"

I chuckled, then looked at Laila Lund, who hadn't moved a muscle in all the time I had been sitting there babbling on. I didn't even know if she was listening to me at all.

"Sorry," I said. "I just needed to unload a little. It's not that I am jealous or anything... well, maybe I am, but I want what's best for him, don't get me wrong; it's just that I feel like I'm losing him a little bit every day. Maybe it's a natural process; I don't know."

I exhaled and looked at my phone between my hands. It was getting late, and I had to head back soon. I was disappointed that Laila Lund hadn't said a word. I knew she was sick, but I had hoped she would at least be able to speak a little, even if what she said probably wouldn't make any sense. I looked at her face, then moved a lock of hair that was blocking her view. She didn't seem to mind though.

"What's it like in there? Does it get lonely?" I asked.

I thought about her when she was younger and how she had lived a life as a nurse, taking care of patients just like herself. Was it life's cruel irony somehow? What went on inside that body? Could she hear me? Was she trying to answer me, but her body wouldn't let her? I couldn't imagine living a life like this, not being able to talk to anyone or even look at them. Was this really a life worth living?

And that was when she finally decided to start to speak. She didn't look at me, but words simply spurted out of her so fast it was hard to find out what it was she was trying to say. It sounded almost like a nursery rhyme the way she almost sang the words.

"Wet critters, drip-drip-drip. Little critters, ha-ha-ha, small little critters crawling up the water, drip-drip-drip. First, we saw the head, then the eyes-eyes-eyes in the water staring up at us. Blink-blink-blink. Little critters in the water, in the pipes, bang-bang-bang, banging all night. Plumber came, hurry-hurry-hurry. Must get the critters out. Ha-ha-ha! First, we saw the hair. That was what we saw, yes-yes-yes, that was what we saw. And then... then the eyes and the nose-nose-nose. Little wet critters, splash-splash-splash, dripping on the floor, drip-drip-drip."

While speaking, Laila Lund was doing something with her fingers, and it reminded me of my own children when we sang

"Itsy Bitsy Spider." She still wore that grin on her face, and her eyes seemed to be rolling around in her head.

Madder than a bat.

The door opened, and the nurse from earlier came in. I looked at her.

"Is she talking about the wet critters again? I feared she might start to do that. I'm so sorry," she said and approached us. "It creeps me out. Maybe we should stop. Besides, Laila needs her nap now."

I rose to my feet. I threw a glance at Laila, who seemed to still be in another world. As the nurse grabbed her chair and turned her around to roll her away, she looked at me one last time, then said, while tilting her head from side to side, "Drip-drop, drip-drop, drip-drop, DEAD!"

THIRTY-FIVE

I made it home just in time to prepare afternoon tea. Victor came through the front door a few minutes later and greeted Skye, who was already waiting for him in the hallway. Me, he didn't even say hello to before he rushed out into the garden, holding Skye's hand in his.

I sighed and returned to the kitchen where my bread was baking in the cooker, and then Maya came home. She slammed the door, and I heard her backpack fall to the floor. I walked out to say hello, but she was already halfway up the stairs.

"Hello?" I said. "Does no one wants to even say hi to their mother?"

Apparently not. Maya was probably still mad about what had happened earlier this morning. I didn't quite understand how I ended up being the bad person in all this when she was the one who had messed up. Maya had a way of turning these things around and making me feel guilty. It was a gift.

Our afternoon tea became strange and very silent. I knocked on Maya's door, but she told me she wasn't hungry and then asked me to go away. So, it was just Victor, Skye, and me. The kids didn't say a word but were obviously communicating on other levels, because they kept snickering and giggling. I don't think I had ever heard Victor snicker before.

"So, how was your day at school?" I asked my son in the hope he would engage just a little with his mother.

He didn't even turn his head in my direction. He just kept staring at Skye and she at him. It was like their minds were locked into each other's and there was nothing else in this world.

This can't be healthy, can it?

"Victor?" I asked. "Victor?"

He still didn't react. It was like he was completely detached from this world, my world, the real world.

The kids rose to their feet, then ran out into the garden again without even a word to me. I sighed and leaned back in my chair, sipping my hot chocolate and finishing my buttered bread with jam. I was wondering about Victor when my thoughts drifted off to earlier this day and my visit with the crazy Laila Lund. I shuddered slightly when thinking about her and those rolling eyes and the words she had said. I was trying to make sense of it, which I kind of knew was impossible, but part of me still desired to.

Wet critters? Dripping on the floor? What did she mean? Critters in the pipes? What kind of critters?

I got up, walked to the bathroom in the hallway, and stood outside, staring at the closed door. I hadn't had been in there since I had seen something slip into the drain, something big and wet. The plumber had told me it could be frogs, but somehow, I didn't think that's what it was. It was something else, and the very notion of it made me shiver. I couldn't escape the thought that I woke up so often at night because the pipes moaned and groaned and sometimes even thumped. What the heck was down there?

Little critters in the water, in the pipes, bang-bang-bang, banging all night.

I shook my head almost violently. This was silly. It was more than that; it was stupid. Ridiculous, even to listen to some crazy woman babbling.

I scoffed and walked back to the kitchen, grabbed the plates, and began to clean up. I was making Danish meatballs—*frikadellers*—for dinner. I put on my apron to start preparing it when there was a knock on my door.

THIRTY-SIX

Hanne shuddered. It wasn't because it was cold inside the restroom. No, the reason for her shivering was the sound of the dripping water. Usually, that sound wouldn't make the hair rise on her neck the way it did now, but these drips were different somehow. They sounded exactly like what she had heard the night before and the one before that. That same sound of water dripping, keeping her awake all night.

Had it followed her to her work?

Nonsense. How would that be possible? Don't be stupid. I'm a woman of science. There's probably just a leak here as well. Someone left a tap on. Don't be silly.

Hanne closed her eyes and imagined herself on Crete with Per. They went there every year in February when the sky was dark gray in Denmark, and the sun barely rose. February was the worst month in this country, Hanne believed, and she always tried to get away. Just to get a few rays of sunlight and maybe a swim in the ocean. She couldn't wait to go again.

Things had been tense at work lately. Ever since they lost the subject. They had all been interviewed about their role and whereabouts on that day when there had been a breach. B-3 had been her subject, her research. And now she was gone. Still, they didn't know whom to blame for the disappearance. No one knew how the subjects managed to get out of this secure location. It seemed impossible, at least they had thought it was.

For days, they had searched for B-3 on the island and around the lab, but B-3 remained gone without a trace. Hanne couldn't quite grasp how the subject would even manage to survive without being seen. The world out there wasn't a place for her. Wouldn't they have heard about it if someone had found her? Hanne believed they would.

When Hanne opened her eyes again, the dripping had stopped. She looked under the door of the booth and realized a puddle had shaped on the floor. A puddle of water.

Hanne gasped, then got up. She pulled up her trousers and opened the door. She stared at the puddle on the floor, then at the sinks. They were pretty far away. How had the water gotten all the way over here? Was there a leak in one of the toilets? But the puddle seemed so round and didn't seem to be connected to any source. Where did the water come from?

Hanne walked around the puddle, then looked toward the sinks again. Maybe there was a pipe somewhere that dripped. As her head remained turned, she heard a small drip coming from behind her, and she turned to look with a gasp. But nothing was there. There were rings in the water though.

Hanne stared at the water moving beneath her, then heard a slow slithering sound coming from above her. Heart pounding, she lifted her glance and looked up.

What she saw up there under the ceiling made her stop breathing. Her first—and final—thought was that of excitement, as the pillar of massive water began gushing down her throat and lungs, being forced explosively inside her body till she slowly suffocated.

THIRTY-SEVEN

"Yes?"

"You don't recognize me?" the man standing outside my door said. "We met... months ago. My wife... Ann?"

My heart skipped a beat. "Oh, dear Lord, I'm so sorry. I didn't recognize you. Brian, right?"

He nodded.

"I'm so sorry; come on in."

"Thank you," he said and followed me inside.

We walked to the kitchen where I served him some hot chocolate and bread with butter and jam. I didn't ask him if he wanted anything but just assumed he needed it. The way I was raised, we didn't let anyone inside our house without feeding them. It was a Danish thing, I guess. And it was impolite for the guest to say no, so it went both ways.

He smiled a sad, yet affirming, smile. "Thank you."

I grabbed a second round myself, and we ate. "So... Brian. First of all, I'm so sorry for your loss."

He took a deep breath like he needed more air for what came next, then nodded. "Thank you."

"How're you holding up?"

"I... I... not so good, to be honest."

"Well, it's a big loss," I said and sipped my hot chocolate. For some reason, I kept hearing my mother's annoying voice in my head telling me not to drink that sugary stuff. She had a way of getting in my head at the most inconvenient times. I ignored it. "And quite unexplainable. Have the police come any closer to figuring out what happened to her?"

"Well... they kind of think I might be involved."

"No!"

"Yes, I'm afraid so. They keep asking me to come to the mainland for questioning. They can't seem to figure out how she landed in our bed when she drowned."

I sipped more of my hot chocolate while looking pensively at him. "It is strange. You have to give them that."

A tear shaped in Brian's eye, and he wiped it away.

"I'm sorry," I said. "I'm making you emotional. That wasn't my intention."

"It's okay," he said. "I had promised myself that I wouldn't cry, but it's... hard. I feel so... guilty."

"That's only natural," I said. "Anyone would feel that way."

"Yeah, well for me, it's a little more than the usual guilt. See... I was with this woman... when... *it* happened."

"A woman? Another woman?"

He nodded. "Yes."

"Ah, I see," I said. "So, you do have an alibi, but not one that you can tell. Is she married too?"

"Yes," he said and bit his lip.

"And she wouldn't confirm your story even if you told it," I said.

"Nope. Can't risk it, she says. She would lose everything."

"But so will you if you go to prison over this," I said.

"Don't think she cares much about that," he said and took a

bite of his bread. A little bit of jam stayed on his upper lip and jiggled up and down as he spoke.

"That's why I've come to you."

THIRTY-EIGHT

"I need your help."

Brian took another bite of his bread.

I gaped at him. "You want my help? How so?"

He exhaled a deeply felt breath. His fingers were tapping on the side of his cup like he was contemplating something.

"I read your book."

I blinked a few times, trying to figure out what he was trying to say. "You read my book? Which one?"

"The latest one."

"*Where the Wild Roses Grow*?" I asked and took a sip from my cup.

He shook his head. "No, the one they're all talking about. *Waltzing Matilda*."

I almost spit out my hot chocolate.

"You read that?"

"Don't be so surprised," he said. "My sister recommended it to me."

I stared at him, not quite knowing what to say. I had done absolutely no advertising for the book and, frankly, I didn't think anyone would read it after what had been said online and in the newspapers. I had hardly even been thinking about it at all after I had doomed it a failed project.

"Your sister? She read it too?" I asked, wrinkling my nose.

"Yes, is that so strange?"

"No... I just... thought... well, I didn't think anyone would read it. Not after what the reviewers wrote about it and about me."

Apparently, I had said something funny because Brian burst into loud laughter.

"Are you kidding me? Everyone is reading it. They all had to see what the fuss was about, and I'm telling you, they like it. When I bought the book, it was number seven on the bestseller list."

My eyes popped. "What?"

"See for yourself."

I grabbed my phone and went to the web page. I scrolled down to the rankings and then looked up at Brian.

"It's number one now."

"There you go. And so well deserved. It's good, Emma. I really liked it. And it is also the reason why I'm here."

I looked down again just to make sure my eyes hadn't betrayed me, but it was still true. The book had more than a thousand reviews, and almost all of them were four or five stars. Most of them praised the book for being fiction and praised me as an author for having a wonderful imagination and for finally sharing it with the world.

How on earth is that even possible?

Brian leaned forward and placed a hand on top of mine. "I need your help finding out who killed my wife. You're my only hope if I want to stay out of prison, the way I see it."

"But... but why me?" I asked, putting the phone down. Lots of news to digest all at once.

"Because you believe in the supernatural. You're the only one I know who does around here."

I swallowed hard. "The supernatural. Why do you say that?"

"Because of your book. I know that most people think the book is fiction, but I don't. Had you asked me a few weeks ago, I would have answered differently, but the more I think about my wife's death, the more I realize something out of this world happened to her."

I cleared my throat. "Why exactly do you say that?"

"Because she drowned in our own darn bed."

I nodded. "Okay. But couldn't someone have placed her there to cast the blame on you? After drowning her, I mean?"

"Yes, that's a valid point," he said, but then there's this." Brian reached into his pocket and pulled out a small container. Inside was what looked like plain water.

"What's this?"

"A sample. There was a puddle on the floor next to the bed when I found her. I took a sample of it and had it analyzed. My wife used to work with stuff like that, so I called up one of her coworkers at the lab and asked for a favor. They came back with this," he said and unfolded a piece of paper. He handed it to me. As I took it, I realized his hand was shaking.

"Read the second line," he said.

My eyes fell on the paper and on the words, but I wasn't sure I understood them. I looked up.

"Human DNA?"

He nodded, holding the container up in the light. "Yes. This water isn't normal water."

"But... how is this possible? How does the water contain human DNA?" I asked and handed the paper back to him.

He shrugged. "I don't know. That's what I was hoping you'd help me find out. Somehow."

I grabbed the container and looked at the water inside it, letting it slide up the sides.

"I've seen this before," I said. "And I'm afraid your wife isn't the only one who has fallen victim to this... whatever it is."

Brian's eyes widened. "Really?"

I shook my head, found my phone, and pulled up an article in the local paper about the death of Sven Thomsen. I showed it to Brian.

"But it says he died of natural causes," he said. "That he had heart problems."

"I was there," I said, "when they found him. And I saw the exact same type of water in a puddle right next to his dead body. My guess is whatever killed your wife went after him too, and who knows... maybe others as well."

"H-how do we figure that out?" Brian asked.

"That's where I come in. If there is anything I'm good at in this world, it's research. Leave that to me."

THIRTY-NINE

Maya felt miserable. She couldn't sit still on her bed, even trying to watch Netflix on her computer; she'd catch her mind wandering away a few seconds later. Even trying to do her homework, she found herself unable to concentrate.

What was going on with her?

She decided to google it. According to the internet, she either had HIV, a concussion, or lead poisoning. It could also be anxiety, another web page suggested, possibly caused by stress. That sounded most plausible to her, so she looked up more about that. After all she had been through... losing her memory, being kidnapped, and almost being killed by a serial killer she believed was her boyfriend, maybe it wasn't so strange to feel a little anxious every now and then.

She was halfway through an article about stress disorder treatment that she had to restart three times because she kept losing her focus when her phone rang. It was Christina.

"Hi there, stranger. What's going on? We hardly spoke at school today. You seemed so distant. Are you okay?"

Maya took a deep breath and looked out the window. "I don't know. I think maybe not. I keep feeling so restless, and I can't concentrate on anything. I tried to read up for the history test tomorrow, but none of the words seem to be sticking. I keep looking out the window, and I don't even know what I'm staring at or what I'm thinking about. I don't know what to do. I'm completely out of it. I can't eat anything either because my stomach feels like a knot. I can't think; it's like I can't be in my own body, I can't... I'm afraid that I'm having an anxiety attack or something. I don't know, I am so confused, I keep checking my phone constantly like I am expecting something, but I don't know what it is, I can't—"

"And exactly what are you thinking about when your mind wanders off?" Christina asked.

"What am I thinking about? I... I don't know..."

"Oh, I think you do."

"I think about this morning, I guess," Maya said.

"Ah, and what exactly happened this morning? Why were you late for school?" Christina asked. "You weren't alone, were you? I mean, both you and Alex were suspiciously late."

Maya sunk down on the bed with a deep sigh. "I guess I am thinking about him and the way he almost... kissed me. I keep running over that same scene again and again, but when I think about it, his lips actually touched mine."

"He kissed you. For real this time?"

"Well... no. I mean, he almost did. My mom came in right when he was about to. But he wanted to. And so did I, I guess..."

"I think I know what's wrong with you," Christina said. "You're in love, my friend."

Maya shot up. "No way."

"Way."

Maya groaned. The butterflies in her stomach did somersaults like they had only been waiting for her to realize this turn of events. For so long Maya had fought this. She really couldn't let it happen to her, could she?

FORTY

Maria Finnerup sipped her second cup of coffee and glanced at the screen in front of her. She looked down at the papers next to her, then wrote another couple of lines in her report.

The trials the day before had been very fruitful, and Maria knew she might be looking at something big here. Years of research seemed to be paying off at last. She was looking at a very big bonus coming her way.

As a child, she had always held a love for the extraordinary, and even as she grew up and placed all her faith in science, she knew that there was more to this world than what she had seen so far.

It had all started when she was no more than eight years old, and she saw a small rock floating in the air on the playground. It had been right in front of her, like it was staring at her, floating about half a meter above the ground. Maria had held her breath and then reached out to grab it, but the rock had moved away fast. It had shot through the air like someone was throwing it, and that was when she thought she saw something else.

It was like there was someone there, someone who she had

later concluded had been holding the rock. But this someone couldn't be seen. As she reached out her hand, she felt something though. It felt like she grabbed a person and that person gasped when she did, but a second later, they was gone.

As Maria reached out her hand to grab them once again, there was nothing there. Maria told everyone on the playground at her school about it, even the teachers, but no one ever believed her. Even so, Maria knew what she had seen and felt.

She knew there was more to this world, and she had dedicated her life to figuring out what. That was how she landed the job at Omicon. She had written an article in *Science Now* about superhumans or the possibility of people visiting from different worlds, parallel universes, people with strength and powers she could only dream of, much to the laughter and mocking of her colleagues. But she had ended up being the last to laugh because that article was how the people behind Omicon discovered her and then contacted her.

She had worked at the lab for twelve years and seen things she could never talk about, but things that would absolutely blow people's minds if they ever knew. But they couldn't know. That was part of the job. The secrecy. She could never reveal her research outside the lab's walls, she was told. But, it was hard when people were mocking her publicly. It was tough not to speak up.

Yet there is a lot about my work I don't want to speak about. A lot I don't even want to think about. The things I have done to get to where I am today.

Maria finished her coffee and realized she had to go to the restroom. She got up from her chair and walked out to the hallway to the women's restroom, then pushed the door open.

The first thing that hit her as strange was the sound of water dripping. The sound soon turned into something slithering, something big and wet sliding away.

But this sound was no stranger to Maria, and as she rushed inside and found her coworker on the floor in a puddle of water, her eyes staring wide open at the ceiling, Maria's heart almost completely stopped. Not so much because she was sad to lose Hanne; no, it was because she knew she could be next.

FORTY-ONE

"They work in the same place."

Morten was eating his potato salad and frikadeller, looking a little distant and only listening to half of what I was telling him.

"What's that? Who does?"

"Are you even listening to me?" I asked and ate another meatball, dipping it thoroughly in the brown sauce.

"Sorry," he said. "Jytte is giving me trouble."

"Now what?" I asked with a sigh.

Morten gave me a look. "Hey. I listen to all your problems with your kids all the time. But, God forbid I even mention my daughter. Of course, my daughter is always the big problem, right?"

I bit my tongue. Me and my big mouth. "Of course, Morten. Of course, you can talk about her. What's going on?"

He exhaled, shaking his head. "I'm sorry. She's just... on my case all the time. She doesn't feel like I am prioritizing her enough. She says I'm here all the time and she's lonely at the house."

I closed my eyes for a second. The girl was nineteen; why was that a problem again? Why didn't she have friends she could hang with? But I didn't say any of this out loud, which I was very proud of.

"Maybe you could do something with her soon," I said, secretly applauding myself for being the bigger person. "You could plan a trip together. How about going for a long weekend to Copenhagen and going shopping or something like that?"

Morten growled. "You know I hate that stuff. Plus, I'm swamped at work. We had another death today. Luckily, Allan took it. I couldn't really deal with more dead people."

"Let me guess," I said. "Someone who works at Omicon?"

Morten gave me a look. "As a matter of fact, it was at Omicon, inside the lab. She was found in the restroom there. How did you know?"

"Well, if you had been listening to what I told you earlier, you'd know I've been doing a lot of research today since Brian Mortensen came here and asked for my help. And what I found out is that they both work or have worked for Omicon."

"What do you mean by both?" he asked. "There was nothing strange about Sven Thomsen's death."

"Well, you never had him autopsied, so how would you know?" I asked.

"It wasn't necessary, according to Dr. Williamsen."

"Seriously? You listen to that old geezer now? I mean, I love Dr. Williamsen, don't get me wrong, but what does he know? I bet if you have Sven Thomsen autopsied, you'll realize he died from drowning too."

"He had a weak heart, Dr. Williamsen said. That's enough for me. He had treated him for it and prescribed him medicine. It wasn't odd that the man died. He had been very upset lately with the neighbors, they told us. And the snow and because his daughter had left the island. It isn't exactly rocket science to figure out that his heart couldn't take it anymore."

"But what about the water, Morten, huh? He was soaked in water, and there was a puddle on the floor. I'm telling you, it's not natural what's going on here. I hear it at night. The pipes are banging and rumbling, and then I wake up because there's dripping coming from my bathroom, but as soon as I go there, it's gone. It disappears back into the drain. I'm telling you, something is going on down there underneath our houses, something strange, and I think that something is killing people."

Morten chuckled and almost spat out his food. "By drowning them? How?"

I leaned back in my chair and sipped my red wine. "I don't know how it works yet, but I'm telling you this. Ann used to work for Omicon and so did Sven. And now you tell me a third person has been killed, inside Omicon. That is the connection. That's what they have in common."

"It's a coincidence," he said and looked away. He didn't want to discuss this anymore; that was obvious.

Because he knew I was right.

FORTY-TWO

I was disappointed that Morten didn't decide to spend the night—again. Instead, he decided to go home right after dinner and be with his daughter. They were going to see a film together. He promised me he would be able to spend the night on the weekend, either Friday or Saturday. He told me this as we kissed goodbye. I pulled him close and tried to plant a kiss that he wouldn't forget anytime soon, but it came off as clumsy and awkward instead. I don't know why. I wasn't angry with him or anything. I was still attracted to him. Wasn't I? I thought so.

As I closed the door behind him, I wondered where we were going with all this. Was this all there was to our relationship? Eating dinners together? Seeing each other a few hours a day? Wasn't it about time we took it to the next level or at least moved forward? I felt like we were constantly going backward lately. Were we drifting apart?

The thought made me shiver, and I rushed into the living room and sat by the fireplace while watching TV for the rest of the evening. I decided to go to bed early, right after tucking in Victor and Skye and leaving Brutus in his usual corner to watch them.

But, of course, I had a hard time falling asleep. I lay awake for hours, wondering about Morten and how tired I was of waiting for him, waiting for us to move ahead. I wanted to. And I had told him that. He wanted it too, he said, but he was afraid of losing his daughter in the process.

I sighed and turned to the side when I once again heard the dripping coming from behind the bathroom door. I stared at it through the darkness, wondering what was going on in there. As it continued for quite a while, I finally rose to my feet. I grabbed my son's baseball bat that he had never used, then walked to the door and placed my hand on the handle. I realized I was shaking heavily as I pushed the door open with a loud bang.

And there it was.

Right in front of me stood something, something I had no words to describe. A creature, looking like it had grown, emerged out of water. I didn't get to have a really good look at it long enough before it disintegrated in front of my eyes and became nothing but water, a puddle on my floor, a puddle that moved fast into the shower and disappeared down the drain with a loud sucking sound.

I stared at the drain where it had gone through, the bat clutched between my hands, ready to swing it should this strange creature show its clear face again. Meanwhile, I couldn't stop thinking about the eyes that had been looking back at me, even though it was for just a split second. I had looked into them and realized this was no animal. There was a brain and a soul behind this, whatever it was. And it terrified me to the core that it had such easy access to my house.

I fell asleep sitting on the bathroom floor, the bat still clenched in my hands and, as my alarm went off the next morning, I woke up with a shriek and looked around with a gasp when my hand touched some water left on the floor. I felt it between my fingers and recognized it as the same I had felt on the floor next to Sven Thomsen. My heart was pounding in my throat as I touched it with my finger, wondering if this monster had also come here to kill me.

I reached down, found the drain plug, and pushed it in. Next, I continued to do the same to each and every drain in the entire house.

FORTY-THREE

It was strange not feeling safe in my own home, staring at every sink in the house as a potential entrance for this monster. While the kids were in school, I kept all the doors closed to the bathrooms, closed the lids on all the toilets, and sat in my kitchen staring at the tap like I expected it to come out of there any minute now. This slimy, wet creature that could turn itself into a puddle of water at any time.

What the heck was it?

I used my laptop to research this strange phenomenon, but most of what I found was about the creature from that film, *The Shape of Water*, which bore no similarities to my water monster. I sure as heck wasn't going to fall in love with it either. Maybe it was a snake of some sort.

I looked it up. But water snakes were nothing compared to what I had seen. Seeking drain monsters resulted in me watching some strange videos taken from a drainage of annelid worms. It made me want to throw up, so I closed the lid of my computer and continued staring at the sink.

Sophia came over a little later and brought pastry from the

bakery. I served her coffee, and we sat down, but I kept staring at the water inside my cup, wondering if this monster could somehow grow out of it and suddenly emerge in front of us, killing us both.

"Are you not going to even drink your coffee?" Sophia finally asked after our second piece of pastry. "What's the matter with you today?"

"I saw the monster," I said, "that is living in our pipes."

"What are you talking about?" she asked.

"You know the noises, the dripping at night, the slithering wet sounds? I saw what it was. Last night. It was in my bathroom. We locked eyes for just a second before it vanished back into my drain. I'm telling you, Sophia, it simply turned itself into water."

"Please, don't tell me you're going to fall in love with it and have weird sex, because that scene in the film was just disgusting. I get sick even thinking about it now."

"Ha-ha. Very funny," I said. "But I'm not making jokes here. I think this water creature is the one killing people on this island. There was another death yesterday, Morten told me. At Omicon. I looked for it this morning, but I can't find anything about it anywhere. Not till I hacked into the police server and read about it. The woman was found inside the restroom of the lab in a puddle of water. They haven't done the autopsy yet, but my guess is they'll find that she drowned."

Sophia almost spit out her coffee. "Drowned? In a restroom? That's a sad way to go."

"The others drowned too. Ann Mortensen in her bed. Sven Thomsen in his recliner."

"How do you drown in your bed or a recliner?" Sophia asked.

I shook my head. "If a water monster attacks you, I guess anything is possible, right?"

Sophia gave me a look. I could tell she didn't believe a word I was saying. She looked more like she was ready to admit me to a mental institution.

"If you say so."

FORTY-FOUR

Saturday, I had invited Victor's new friend, Daniel, over to the house. It might have been an attempt to get him away from Skye a little, or maybe just me being totally excited about the fact that he had made a real friend. I don't know, but I thought it was worth a try.

His mother brought Daniel over at ten o'clock and knocked on my door. I hurried and opened it.

"Hello. I'm Emma," I said and shook the mother's hand. I looked at the boy. "You must be Daniel."

The boy smiled shyly. To my surprise, he looked me straight in the eyes when I spoke and, when I reached out my hand to greet him, he shook it. I hadn't expected this because I thought he would be a lot more like Victor and Skye, but this kid seemed very different. His clear and very blue eyes looked up at me.

This kid could be a good influence on my son.

"Come on inside," I said, smiling from ear to ear.

His mother followed him inside and closed the door behind her. Victor and Skye were sitting in the living room like I had asked them to. I had told them not to go into the garden after breakfast like they usually did because Daniel was coming.

Victor hardly reacted when I told him his friend was coming over, and I kept asking him if he was looking forward to seeing him, but he didn't answer me at all. Looking at the boy standing next to his mother, I sincerely hoped he could rub off just a little bit on my son.

"Now... Daniel doesn't like surprises," the boy's mother said, still standing in the hallway, seeming like she almost wasn't sure she dared to leave her son. I knew the feeling. I couldn't stand leaving Victor in new places where I didn't know what might set him off.

"So, please make sure nothing upsets him. Otherwise, call me. I'll be back in an hour."

I smiled and nodded at his mother while looking into her worried eyes. "I will."

The mother stood for a few seconds, shifting the weight on her feet, hand on the doorknob. Then she exhaled and opened it.

"See you in an hour," I said and waved.

As the door closed and the mother disappeared, I turned around and found Daniel standing right behind me. I took his hand in mine and guided him into the living room.

Victor and Skye were sitting on the floor in front of the fireplace, staring into each other's eyes, not making a sound.

"Victor?"

He didn't react.

"Daniel is here."

Still nothing.

"Victor!"

Finally, Victor turned his head. He didn't look up at us but rose to his feet and walked to Daniel. He stood in front of him, his head still bowed. Behind him, Skye was staring at Daniel, and I noticed with concern that her little body was shaking. Daniel spotted her and their eyes locked.

"Do you two know each other?" I asked, surprised.

Biting his lip, Daniel nodded.

"Really?" I said. "Do you know her name?"

He nodded shyly. "B-3."

I shook my head in wonder. "B-3? What do you mean?"

"B-3," he repeated.

I looked down at him. "Daniel. Where do you know her from?"

He looked up at me, blue eyes growing even wider. "From the place with the cords. The place where no one hears you scream."

And with those words, Daniel let go of my hand, then rushed to Skye and embraced her. I wanted to stop them I wanted to ask him more questions, but all three of them seemed to soon be lost in some conversation I could never be a part of and, seconds later, they rushed into the garden.

FORTY-FIVE

I spent the morning sitting by the window, watching the kids playing outside in the snow while researching on my computer. I had read all there was about the disappearance of plumber John Andersen and all there was about the company Omicon and what it did. According to its website, it was a research lab, testing and developing new treatments for diabetes patients.

But what struck me was that I couldn't seem to find any of their research online. No articles about some breakthrough the scientists had or were trying to make, no scientific magazine describing their research and work. I told myself that could be because it was top secret or maybe because they hadn't really had any breakthroughs, but there was something about their secrecy that made me curious.

So far, three people who had worked there or were working there had died under strange circumstances. I didn't care what Morten said about it being a coincidence. In my book, something odd was up, something I couldn't really put my finger on.

I was pleased to see that the three kids seemed to play well together and Victor and Skye included Daniel just fine. They didn't seem to really play much, though. At least not that I could tell. Instead, it seemed they were communicating with one another and possibly with the trees. Maybe it was just part of some role play, I decided and returned to my computer.

I looked up the latest death, Hanne Carlsen. Her autopsy report concluded—not surprisingly—that she had water in her lungs and in her stomach, indicating death by drowning. The water had caused loss of consciousness due to hypoxia and was followed by cardiac arrest. The report stated she was found on the floor of the restroom, in the middle of the room, far from any outlets containing water. It had to be a result of submersion injuries, was the conclusion. I looked it up and found it was also known as secondary drowning.

According to an article I found, secondary drowning happened when a little bit of water got into the lungs of a person and caused inflammation or swelling, making it difficult or impossible for the body to transfer oxygen to carbon dioxide. With secondary drowning, there could be a delay of up to twenty-four hours before the person showed signs of distress.

"So, that's their theory, huh?" I said out loud. "That she somehow was exposed to water somewhere else, then walked into the restroom at her work and died there on the floor."

I leaned back in the couch with a deep sigh, wondering about all this. Could they be right? Could someone have tried to drown Hanne? Could the same thing have happened to Ann Mortensen and Sven Thomsen? But what about the puddles? There were puddles on the floor next to Sven Thomsen and Ann Mortensen. Puddles with that strange water in them. Water that, according to Brian Mortensen, contained human DNA.

I sighed. It was all a little too farfetched. I closed the lid of the computer and looked at the kids while sipping my coffee, wondering about Daniel. If he knew Skye, did that mean that she was originally from the island?

There was a knock on the door, and I hurried to answer it.

Outside stood Daniel's mother, and I realized the hour had passed.

"They're in the garden," I said and let her in.

We walked to the living room, and I turned to look at her. "Say... Daniel, how long has he been at Fishy Pines?"

She exhaled. "He's been there since he started school. Used to be there full-time, but now he only goes for the classes. We knew something was off with him from when he was just a young baby."

"So, does he know all the children who have gone there?" I asked.

"Yes. That place has been like a second home to him for as long as I can remember," she said.

I opened the door to the garden and glanced at the woman next to me. "That's wonderful. It'll be good for Victor to know someone like Daniel. Someone who's familiar with how things work there. You know because he's so new."

"Yes, of course."

We stepped out on the back porch. I shuddered in the cold, then waved at the kids.

"Victor. Daniel's mom is here."

Daniel spotted her and rose to his feet. He gave Skye a hug, then ran toward us.

"Say... who is that girl?" his mother said.

"You know her?" I asked. "How so?"

"I don't know," the mother said. "What's her name?"

I suddenly had a strange sensation inside of me and realized I wasn't sure I wanted people to know about Skye being in my house. What if they took her away from me? It would devastate Victor. What if they hurt her?

"Skye," I said. "She's visiting from out of town. Distant relatives."

"Oh, really?" the mother said.

"Yes," I said, suddenly eager to get them out of my house. I liked the boy, I really did, but the mother and the way she stared at Skye suddenly gave me the creeps.

"All right then, Daniel," she said. "We better be off. What do we say to Miss Frost?"

"Thank you, Miss Frost," Daniel said, sounding like a little robot.

I smiled and pulled the boy into a hug, enjoying the fact that he didn't start screaming like my own son.

"Call me Emma," I said. "And promise me you'll come again soon, you hear me?"

He nodded with another of his adorable smiles. For a second, I wondered what he was even doing at Fishy Pines. He seemed nothing like Victor. But then again, there were many things kids could have to deal with these days and not all of them were obvious.

"Thank you, Emma," the mother said and shook my hand before they left. As I watched them get into her minivan in my driveway, Skye came up to me and stood beside me. She stared at the woman as she got into her car, then stuck out her tongue at her.

That made me laugh.

FORTY-SIX

"I can't believe you're going with Alex to Thomas K's party. You're going to be the talk of the town; you do realize that, right?"

Maya looked at Christina. They were both standing in front of her open wardrobe, looking at her clothes. Maya had called her and asked her to come over and help her pick out something to wear. Maya had absolutely no idea about fashion or what boys liked.

"You need to look absolutely amazing. If you're to be the couple who everyone envies, we can't have him outshine you. He is so handsome that you have to look even better, so people won't wonder why on earth he is into you. This is important, you hear me?"

Maya nodded, even though she thought it sounded silly. It wasn't like she cared that much about what people thought. She liked Alex, and he wanted to take her to the party. That was all there was to it. Still, Christina insisted that this was their first appearance together and that held great significance, so it had to be just perfect. Maya was about to regret her decision even to go when Christina pulled out a dress from the wardrobe.

"There's always the little black one. You can never go wrong with a black dress. Black is timeless and slimming."

"But isn't it a little boring?" Maya asked.

"It's classy."

Maya sighed and looked at her old dress. "It used to be my mom's," she said. "She gave it to me when she went through her stuff a few years ago and realized she could no longer fit into most of it."

"I think you should wear it," Christina said. "Alex will love it. Try it on."

Maya took the dress and put it on. She looked at herself in the full-size mirror, then turned a few times to see it from all sides.

"I don't know..." she said.

"It's perfect," Christina decided. "We'll put your hair up in a bun. It will look gorgeous with your blonde hair as a contrast to the black dress."

"I look kind of pale."

"That's because you are pale," Christina said. "But that's part of your beauty. Like a fragile flower."

Maya chuckled. She had never seen herself as being fragile or even flowerlike.

"I have some earrings you can borrow," Christina said. "And some heels."

"I don't want to be too dressed up," Maya said. "What if the others come wearing jeans?"

"Then you'll be the prettiest of them all, won't you?" Christina said.

Maya smiled nervously. She never really liked going to parties and was only doing this to be with Alex. She hadn't been able to think about anything else since that kiss they had almost shared in her kitchen. It was driving her crazy. She had never felt this way about anyone before.

"Come on; let's put some makeup on that face, shall we?" Christina said.

Maya sighed and did as she told her to, then closed her eyes. While Christina painted her eyes and made her look everything but herself, she wondered what she expected to get out of this night. She didn't have to think about it hard or long. She knew exactly what she dreamt and hoped for.

A kiss. A real kiss this time. Not a forced one or one that only almost happened. A real one.

FORTY-SEVEN

I had just sent Maya off to a party with her new boyfriend. Alex picked her up at our house, while her friend Christina took off, riding her bike through the snow back to her own house. Right after they had all left, Morten came over, a tired look on his face.

I kissed him and closed the door behind him. "I have chicken in the cooker."

I wondered for a second if I should tell him what had happened today, that I believed Daniel knew Skye and that she somehow was connected to Fishy Pines, but then decided against it. I didn't want to get into an argument. Morten would only try to persuade me to go to the authorities with the girl as he had tried so many times before. For once, we had a night ahead of us, just us, and I wanted it to be about that and nothing else.

"That's the most romantic thing anyone has said to me all day," he chuckled and took off his thick coat.

I grimaced and ran into the kitchen to check on the chicken. It smelled heavenly but wasn't quite done yet. Morten came out, and I poured him a glass of wine. He took it, then put it down. He grabbed me by the shoulders and pulled me into a long, deep kiss. I closed my eyes and enjoyed it, tasting him.

"Wow. What was that for?" I asked when his lips left mine.

He looked into my eyes. "Not for anything. I just wanted to kiss you; that's all."

He let go of me and grabbed his glass of wine. He took a big sip. I could hear him swallow.

"Well, it was nice," I said and grabbed my own glass and clinked it against his.

"So, are your parents eating with us tonight?" he asked.

I shook my head and sipped my wine. "Nope. Just gonna be the two of us. And Victor and Skye, of course."

"That's nice," he said.

"So, how was your day?" I asked and began making the sauce. "Any more deaths among workers from Omicon?"

"Very funny," he said.

"Do you still think it's a coincidence?"

He shrugged. "Not really my job to figure out, is it? I'll let the detectives from the mainland do that part."

"So, what have they found out so far?" I asked.

"You know I can't tell you that. Besides, if I know you right, you've already read the latest report, haven't you? Actually, don't tell me. I don't want to know. If you break the law, keep it to yourself, please."

I smiled while stirring the sauce. "What do they do at Omicon anyway?" I asked.

Morten shrugged. "Something with diabetes, I heard. Finding new ways to treat it, or... I don't know."

"I can't seem to find out much on the internet. They keep it very quiet," I said.

"Well, I guess that kind of research can be worth a lot of money. You know how the medical industry is. They can't risk someone else stealing their research."

I nodded as the cooker dinged. I opened it and took out the

chicken. Morten's face lit up when he saw it. Chicken was one of his favorite dishes.

"Looks really good, Emma," he said as I placed it on the table. He glanced briefly at his watch.

"You in a hurry?" I asked.

He shook his head. "No. No. It's just..."

He paused, and I felt my heart drop. I had a feeling I knew what would come next.

"Just what, Morten?"

He sighed. "Well... I kind of... I promised Jytte I'd watch a film with her tonight."

I dropped the spoon in my hand. "You did what?"

Morten sighed and put his glass down. "I knew you'd be mad. Emma. Don't be angry, please... she needs me."

"She needs you. Again? What, she needs you every night now? I thought you were spending the night here. I thought we would spend the morning in bed together tomorrow."

"And I really want that, Emma. I really do... but it's just she—"

"She comes first. I get it," I said and took off my apron. "And I am always second. Always. It's never going to change, is it?"

"Emma... she needs me."

"She's nineteen, Morten. I don't think sleeping alone in the house for one night is going to kill her."

"I'm worried about her, Emma. I don't think she's well."

I shook my head with a scoff. "She's totally playing us out against each other. Don't you see it? She keeps doing this because she knows you can't say no to her. She knows she can manipulate you into choosing her. She never wanted us to be together. Don't you think I know that by now? She never accepted me in your life, and she will do anything to destroy what we have. And, worst of all, you're letting her; you're allowing her to come between us."

"Emma, that's not fair. She's not well... I'm telling you, she's been—"

"You know what? Just go. Go home and be with her. But I can't keep doing this, Morten. If I can't be your number one at least every now and then, then... then I'm done."

"Don't say that, Emma. I can't... I won't... I love you, dammit."

Morten grabbed my arm and pulled me close. He looked into my eyes, and I felt like crying. I loved him so much too, but I just couldn't keep doing this. I couldn't keep hoping for things to get better.

"Don't leave me, Emma. I wouldn't be able to bear it." He spoke with deep desperation in his voice.

I sighed, then stroked his cheek gently with my hand. "Then don't leave tonight. Stay here with me."

Morten exhaled. He thought it over for a few seconds, then nodded. "All right. I'll stay. "

I smiled and leaned over and placed a kiss on his lips while whispering, "Someone's about to get very lucky tonight. It'll be worth it; don't you worry."

FORTY-EIGHT

Maria couldn't find rest in her own house. Seeing Hanne on the floor of that restroom two days earlier had stirred something up in her. Of course, it had. She had heard about Ann and Sven being found dead in their own homes but hadn't seen a connection between their deaths and chalked it up to mere coincidence. Strange, yes, but nothing but two freak deaths that happened to be two of her former coworkers.

But as she stared at Hanne on the floor and saw the puddle next to her, she knew this was no accident; this was no coincidence. This was her past coming back to haunt her.

Maria looked at her hands, holding them above the sink. The toilet was still running from her flushing just a minute ago. Maria's hands were shaking as she turned on the tap. She washed her hands so fast she barely touched the water before she turned it off again. She had placed a chair on top of the toilet to keep the lid closed when she wasn't using it and after the water had run down the drain in the sink, she closed it up, so nothing could come up through the sink.

Maria looked at her face in the mirror. She hadn't been sleeping much since they had found Hanne. She would lie awake at night, listening to the tap dripping in the bathroom or the pipes banging, wondering if the monster would come for her next. But so far, she had managed to keep it out by plugging every drain and closing the lid on every toilet in the house. Her children believed she had lost her mind, but so be it. At least Christopher wasn't home to see her like this. He had left on a business trip to California and wouldn't be home till next week. Hopefully, it would all be over by then. Hopefully.

Maria walked out of the bathroom, walking backward, keeping a close eye on all drains and taps. Once outside, she closed the door quickly and rushed into her kitchen where she had stoppered all the drains as well.

"What's for dinner?" her son asked when she got there. He was sitting by the table, drawing.

She stared at the boy, then forced a smile. "Spaghetti. Your favorite."

The boy didn't even look up or smile when she told him. He continued drawing. She wondered if she should ask him to sleep in her bedroom tonight. Just in case. The monster wouldn't touch her if he was there, would it?

But she knew he wouldn't do it. He was too old to be sleeping in her bed. Not that he ever did it before either. Not like his older brother, whom she could barely get out of her bedroom.

"You hungry now?" Maria asked.

The boy nodded, still without looking up.

"All right. I'll start."

Maria grabbed a pan and walked to the tap and put her hand on the handle, then hesitated. She stood for a few seconds staring at it before she finally turned it on and filled the pot. Hurriedly, she closed it again, rushed to the cooker, and started to boil the water. She stared for a long time at the water in the pot, waiting for it to boil, praying it wouldn't attack her.

As the bubbles emerged from the bottom, she finally

breathed like usual once again. This was just normal water. Had it been the monster, it would have shown its face by now. It only survived in cold or lukewarm water. Burning hot water would have made it jump out. Maria knew that much about it. She knew a lot about it, as a matter of fact.

Too much.

Maria walked to the fridge and pulled out some ground beef to make the sauce. As she turned her head back, she spotted her son standing by the sink, turning on the tap. Water splashed down on top of his hands and ran into the drain. Maria's eyes grew big and fearful. She dropped the meat and ran toward him and turned the tap off, pushing him aside in the process.

"Are you insane?" she panted.

"My fingers were dirty," he said. "From the marker."

Maria stared at him, then down at the water in the sink. She stuck her hand inside and unclogged it, so the water could disappear down the drain. Heart in her throat, she waited for it to disappear, constantly imagining a claw-like hand coming up from beneath it, grabbing her.

Once the water was finally out, she hurried and plugged the drain once again, finally able to breathe.

FORTY-NINE

The atmosphere at dinner was a little tense. I don't think Victor and Skye even noticed because they pretty much stayed in their own little world and didn't communicate with the rest of us at all, but it was tense between Morten and me. He had called Jytte and told her he was staying, stating, "Something came up." But Jytte wasn't stupid. She knew he was with me, she said, and then she had yelled at him angrily, to the point where I could hear her even if I stood at the other end of the kitchen.

It tortured Morten, and he wasn't really present as we ate the chicken and potatoes in cream sauce. He hardly said a word, and his mind seemed to drift off again and again. I wondered how that girl had gotten such a hold on her father at this age and when he would stand up to her and tell her it was time she let him live his life. He was allowed to date; he was allowed to have a girlfriend and have some fun in his life. She was old enough to take care of herself.

But it was easy enough for me to see through the situation and her; I knew it was a lot harder when he was actually in it and when it was his own child.

"You want some more potatoes?" I asked, then looked at his plate. He had barely touched them.

Morten smiled. "I'm good, but thanks."

"You like it? It's a new recipe," I said and took a second helping, enjoying the fact that my mother wasn't around to give me one of her looks. Morten could from time to time give me a hard time too, but not tonight. Tonight, he was too preoccupied with his own problems to worry about my weight and health issues.

"What's that?" he said and looked at me. "Oh, this. Yes, it's really good, Emma. Really."

He shoveled a forkful into his mouth, then chewed, smiling. I could tell he was putting up a show for me, but I wasn't sure I appreciated it. Victor and Skye finished eating, then rushed out of the kitchen and into the living room without a word. I missed hearing my son's voice and actually communicating with him, but since Skye came along, it was like he didn't need me at all, nor did he need to speak. It was better than him screaming at night like he used to, and I sensed that he wasn't having as many nightmares as before he met her, but still. He couldn't stop speaking altogether.

"You don't have to pretend, you know?" I said and ate a bite from the chicken thigh.

Morten rubbed his forehead. "I'm not. I'm sorry. It's just... she sounded so upset."

I sighed. "Listen. I don't want to keep you here against your will. You're free to go if you need to get home to her."

He shook his head and placed his hand on top of mine. "No. Emma. No. I'm here now. I'm here with you. Jytte has to wait. You're the love of my life, and you're perfectly right; it's time I show it."

I exhaled, relieved. I was happy that he prioritized me, really thrilled, but it also filled me with a huge load of guilt.

Morten looked into my eyes. "I want to be here. I really, truly do."

He lifted his glass, and we clinked them. "To us," he said.

"To us," I said.

We drank and put the glasses down.

"I have an idea," he said.

"Uh-huh?" I said, chewing.

He leaned forward and looked deep into my eyes. "What do you say we move in together?"

I choked and began to cough. I grabbed my glass of water and drank from it, while a gazillion thoughts rushed through my mind. Yes, that was what I wanted, but like this? I wasn't sure. It seemed to be coming from him more out of guilt than out of what he really wanted.

"What about Jytte?" I asked, still coughing.

"I'll help her find a place of her own. A condo downtown or something like that. I can help her financially at first just till she gets things up and running."

"I thought she was going away to college?" I asked.

He shook his head. "I don't think it will happen. Every time I mention it, she gets angry with me. I think she needs time. Maybe a year or so off to figure out what she really wants. I did the same."

I stared at Morten, not exactly knowing what to say to him. This is what I wanted; oh, how it was. But was he doing it because he wanted to or because I had persuaded him to, and he wanted to make me happy? Was this what he wanted?

"What do you say?" he asked. "I could sell my house and move in here. There's room enough for both me and the cats."

"That's right," I said. "I forgot you had cats."

Because you never invite me over to your place.

"I'm sure they'll do fine with Kenneth and Brutus," he said chuckling.

"Kenneth will skin them alive," I said with a light gasp.

He sipped his wine, still smiling. "Oh, what the heck. Maybe Jytte can take them, huh? We'll figure it out, right? This is what you want, right?"

"It is..."

"But... why do I sense there's a but coming?" he asked, concerned.

I shook my head. "No. No. No buts... only... I want to make sure this is what you want too."

"YES! It is what I want. Heck, Emma, I've wanted this since we met each other. I could think of nothing better than to be living here... with you and those... odd kids and weird dogs."

I took a deep breath. I didn't know whether to laugh or cry.

"So, what do you say?" he asked.

"I... I..."

He made a face. "Please?"

I exhaled happily. "All right. I guess we're moving in together."

Morten made a happy sound, then leaned over and kissed me again, just as there was a rapid and quite violent knock on my door.

FIFTY

All eyes were on them when Maya and Alex arrived at the party. The music was loud, but all the chatter stopped, and everyone turned their heads to look at them. All eyes followed their every move, observing and judging them, sizing them up.

Maya blushed and kept close to Alex as she walked inside Thomas K's house, staggering along on her high heels. She looked around at the staring faces and realized, to her horror, that everyone else was wearing jeans, and here she was in her little black dress.

Alex had thought she looked beautiful. He had told her when he picked her up in the Uber that took them to the party. He had smiled boyishly and held her hand in his and told her he was looking forward to showing her off to the others. They were going to be so jealous, he had said.

Now, he was no longer holding her hand as they walked into the living room and Thomas K came over to greet them.

"Alex!"

Thomas K didn't greet Maya. He gave her a look, then returned his focus to Alex.

"Let's have a beer, man."

Not knowing what else to do, Maya followed them out into the kitchen when Thomas K turned and looked at her. The look in his eyes made Maya's skin crawl.

"Not you," he said.

"Sorry," Alex told her. "The guys want to chat. No girls. You know how it is. I'll be back in a second, okay?"

Maya swallowed, not knowing what to say. She nodded nervously. "Okay."

He sent her another of his endearing smiles before disappearing with his friends, laughing. Meanwhile, Maya went back into the living room. She looked around her and realized she knew no one there. Well... she knew them because they were all from her school, but there was no one there whom she ever talked to. These were all popular kids. The ones who went to parties like this. The ones who hung with guys like Alex.

What am I doing here? I'll never be anything like them.

She found a couch and sat down while the chattering and loud music continued around her. There was a group of girls who Maya had often seen hang around Alex at school standing close to where she sat. They kept turning their heads to stare at her. Someone said something, and the rest laughed. The way they looked at her made her feel uncomfortable.

I should never have come.

An hour passed and still Alex hadn't come out of the kitchen. Maya was on her phone, going through her Facebook feed or texting Christina, who constantly asked how she was doing, if the party was fun. Maya told her it was okay, mostly because she had been so excited for Maya, she didn't want to spoil it. And the party was okay. She had more fun at home, but it wasn't terrible either.

At some point, she got up from the couch. A couple of girls were dancing, and she walked past them toward the bathroom. As she arrived at the door, there was a line, so she waited. Standing close to the kitchen, she could hear the boys talking.

"Why are you with that girl?" someone asked. "There's something seriously wrong with her."

"I heard she has a mental illness," another guy said.

"You mean she's cuckoo?" a third voice said.

His remark made the others laugh.

"Come on, man," the first voice said. "You can have any girl at the school. Anyone. You can do so much better. Why are you hanging out with that one?"

Maya's heart dropped when listening to them. That one? Was that how they saw her? Like someone with a mental illness? Just because she had memory loss?

Maya felt like she was about to cry and left the line to the bathroom, then rushed back into the living room with the intention of leaving. But she never made it as far as the door. Instead, she ran right into the group of girls from earlier. They shaped a half circle around her, making it hard to get around them.

"Hi there, Maya," a girl named Lene said. "Say, you don't look so good. Are you all right?"

Maya nodded and pushed back tears. "I'm fine."

"You're not leaving already, are you?" she asked. "The party is just getting started."

Maya nodded. "I think... I need to—"

"No. Not when we're just getting to know each other. Why don't you stick around a little longer? Get the party going."

"I can't... I have to go," Maya said.

"But certainly not without having a drink first," Lene continued. "Right, girls?"

"No, you can't leave without at least having a drink," another girl from Maya's class named Anina said.

"What would people say?" Lene said.

Maya stared at her. Lene stretched out her hand where she was holding a plastic cup.

"Here."

Maya stared at the cup, then at the group around her. All

eyes were fixed on her, anticipating her reaction. Maya knew why they were doing this. Because they knew she didn't drink. They knew she would say no and then they could mock her for being such a dork.

But not this time. No, Maya was sick of playing nice. She was sick of being the dull one. She grabbed the cup and started to drink, guzzling it down. All the girls' eyes were on her; some were laughing and, as soon as the liquid hit her tongue, she realized why.

Maya almost choked, then began to spit on the carpet below her. The girls recoiled so they wouldn't get hit.

"What the heck is that?" she yelled, startled.

All the girls broke into laughter, some turning their heads away. Lene grabbed the cup out of Maya's hand. Triumphantly, she leaned close to Maya and said, "That was my urine."

"What?"

"That'll teach you to stay away from Alex."

As she said the words, she swung the cup toward Maya and the rest of the urine was thrown all over Maya's dress.

Maya let out a loud shriek. The cup landed on the carpet, and Lene stepped on it as she and her gang left Maya, giggling and pointing their fingers at her. Maya stayed behind, staring after them, biting hard on her own lip to not start crying. Then she turned around and ran outside. She didn't care that she had no way of getting home. She'd walk if she had to, even if it meant freezing to death. She hurried out and slammed the door behind her, then let out all the tears while beginning to walk home in the snow.

Seconds later, she heard the door slam once again.

"Maya!"

It was Alex. She heard him call, but Maya was so angry she didn't stop. She kept walking up the driveway, and Alex came up behind her.

"Maya, please stop."

She turned around to face him. "Was it all a part of your plan, huh? You never wanted to be with me, did you? Was that why you wanted to bring me here, huh? So they could humiliate me? Was it all part of your plan?"

Alex looked surprised.

"No! Maya. How could you think such a thing? As soon as I heard what they had done, I yelled at them. I got so mad, Maya, you won't believe it. Then I came out here to find you." He paused, then grabbed her hand in his. "Maya. I am so, so sorry. I had no idea they would do this to you. You must believe me."

Maya swallowed, then pressed back more tears, but it was too hard, and she had to let them go. Alex came close to her and put his coat around her. He lifted her chin up and made her look into his eyes.

"I swear, Maya. I didn't know."

"All those nasty things they said... why did they say them?"

"They're morons," Alex said. "All of them. And they're jealous. I mean, look at you. You're gorgeous; you way outdressed everyone there. And you did that for me. We don't need them, Maya. I, for one, am never going to hang out with them again. Any of them. I want to be with you, Maya. I don't care what they say."

"Really?" Maya said with a loud sniffle.

"Yes. You're the best thing that has happened to me... since... well, since ever."

He put his arm around her shoulder. "Come. Let's go back to my place. I don't live far from here. We can walk there. You can take a shower at my house. I'm sure my mom has some clothes you can borrow. Come on, Maya. Let's get out of here."

FIFTY-ONE

The knock intensified and I rushed toward the door. Kenneth barked and growled.

"I'm coming; I'm coming, geez," I complained and opened the door.

Outside stood three men I had never seen before. They wore long dark coats like they had just stepped out of *The Matrix* film. No sunglasses, though. I could see their eyes and faces, but that didn't make me feel any better. Their faces looked like they were taken out of a film too. Stern, icy cold eyes, and I could almost see the muscles underneath those heavy black coats.

"Miss Frost?" the middle guy asked.

My eyes grew wide. "Y-yes?"

"We need to talk to you."

"O-okay?"

He pulled out a picture on his phone and showed it to me. It was a picture of Skye and, as I saw it, my heart dropped.

"We're looking for this girl."

I looked at the picture while contemplating what to do. I had never been good at lying; people could usually see right through me. That was why I never played poker. I had to come up with a face that was believable.

"I... I've never seen her before, I'm afraid. Is she lost?" I asked. I could hear how my voice became shrill and cursed myself for being so incredibly see-through.

"We have reason to believe that she's here," he said and put the phone away.

"Probable cause," the guy next to him said.

"Eyewitness testimony," the third man said.

"Really?" I said, playing along. "Well, I only have a son that age, so—"

"We never told you how old she was," the one in the middle said.

"Well... well... I... I guessed it from the picture. I am a mother you know, heh-heh. We know that stuff."

Stop talking, you moron, please!

"We need you to give us the girl," the middle man said.

"What girl? I don't have any girl."

"As I said, we have reason to believe you do," he said, his voice growing increasingly more serious.

"But I don't," I continued. "Why would I have an extra kid? I have enough kids of my own."

"We don't think this is amusing," the middle man said.

"I can tell," I said.

"Give us the girl," the man to the right said.

I shook my head and wrinkled my forehead. "I told you, I don't have her here. Now, would you please leave? I'm trying to have a nice evening with my boyfriend."

"We'll leave as soon as you give us the girl."

"Well, that's gonna be pretty hard since I don't have her."

"We have reason to believe you do," the middle man repeated.

"We're not really getting anywhere here, are we?" I said. "You have to start paying attention to what I say. I. Don't. Have.

Her. Now, if you'll please leave so I can get back to my boyfriend. We were having a great time until you guys came along. He told me we should move in together. I'll have you know that I am very excited, and I am not letting you ruin that."

"As soon as you hand us the girl," the middle man said.

I stared at them, then sighed and put my hands on my hips. "Say... who are you? Because I don't recall you identifying yourselves."

"Our identity doesn't matter."

"Well, you're not the police; I know that much."

"We could be the police," the guy to my left said.

"You can't just decide to be the police. Is this guy for real?" I asked.

"We just need the girl," the middle man said. He sounded like a robot, and I was beginning to wonder if he was one.

"Please, just leave, will you?"

"Not without the girl."

"She's not here. And I've run out of time and patience with you people. Go somewhere else and harass someone else," I said and started to close the door when the man in the middle reached out and grabbed the door in his hand. He pushed it open with almost no effort, and I was pushed back inside the hallway. When he let go of the door, I noticed his hand had left finger marks in the wood where he had grabbed it.

These guys were no joke.

"The girl," the middle man said and stepped closer.

"No," I said, feeling very intimidated by this guy's size. Especially having him so close to me. "Go away."

The man then reached out his gloved hand and grabbed me by the throat. I could hardly breathe as he lifted me off the ground, just as Morten came out into the hallway.

"What the heck is going on here?"

Morten was still in his uniform, so as soon as the man saw

him, he let go of me, and I fell to the floor, coughing and gasping for air.

"Who are you people?" Morten asked, looking at their faces. "I haven't seen you around here before."

The man didn't reply. He looked down at me, giving me a look to let me know this wasn't over yet before he turned around and walked out to his friends. Morten followed them into the driveway, but they were already gone as he got out there.

Morten closed the door and locked it, then knelt next to me. "Are you okay?"

I sniffled and sat up. I felt my throat. It was sore. "I think so."

"That guy left a bruise on your neck. I can't believe it. I should have arrested them while I had the chance."

I nodded. "Yeah, well, I have a feeling you might get a second chance to do just that."

I rose to my feet, and Morten helped me get back into the kitchen. "Who were they, Emma? What did they want?"

I sat in a chair and sighed, then looked up at him. "Skye. They wanted Skye. And I have a feeling they're willing to go very far to get her."

FIFTY-TWO

Maya was still crying when they reached Alex's house. She couldn't help herself. Never had she been so humiliated in her entire life.

"Here," Alex said and showed her upstairs. "This is my room."

Maya followed him inside and was surprised to see that his room was filled with anime posters and Death Note knick-knacks. Death Note was also Maya's favorite anime, but she had never met anyone else who loved it as much as she did. That made her smile.

"What?" he asked, surprised.

She shook her head. "Nothing."

"But I made you smile. That is, at least, something."

She nodded. "It sure is."

He chuckled, still with his eyes lingering on her face.

"What?" she asked.

Now it was his turn to shake his head. "Nothing. You just have a beautiful smile; that's all."

"I do not," she said.

"Why do you do that?" he asked.

"Do what?"

"Every time I give you a compliment or say something nice, you act like I don't mean it. You really don't know how pretty you are, do you? Or how amazing you are?"

That made Maya quiet. She looked into his eyes while biting her lip. She didn't want to tell him the truth, but the truth was that she was so scared to believe in compliments or believe in boys because she had tried believing them before and been so crudely disappointed. It made her think that there was always an ulterior motive when someone said something nice to her. She always looked for a hidden agenda, for ways they might hurt her. She had learned not to trust anyone.

"Let me find you a towel and some clean clothes," he said and moved into the hallway.

Maya stood for a few seconds and could smell the urine on her dress. She couldn't believe a guy like Alex still wanted to be with her. She had never been more disgusting and yet he had just told her she was pretty.

"Here you go," he said and handed her the stuff. "I found some old jeans and a shirt. It might be a little big because you're smaller than my mom, but it was the best I could do."

"I'm sure it'll be fine," she said.

"The shower is in here," he said and grabbed her hand. He pulled her toward the door and down the hallway, then opened a door and turned on the lights.

Maya chuckled as she walked inside. "What's going on here?"

Alex sighed deeply. "I am sorry. My mom is a little paranoid lately." He grabbed the chair on top of the toilet and removed it. Then he walked to the shower and unplugged the drain and removed the plastic bag that was tied around the tap.

"There you go," he said. "Now, you can shower."

"Why does she do that?" Maya asked.

"What, the chair and plugging of drains and taps? Well, my

mom seems to believe something can come out of it and kill us all while we sleep. I don't really know. Guess we can't all have cool moms like yours, huh?"

Maya chuckled. "She's not always cool. By far not. She's been freaking out about our drains lately too. She thought she saw something in our bathroom downstairs the other day and had a plumber come out and everything. She completely freaked out. The plumber said it might just be frogs or some other animal, but she's still not convinced he's right. She can get crazy. Not to mention my brother, who is so scared of going to the bathroom that he'll hold it in for so long he almost hurts himself."

Maya gasped lightly when realizing she had just shared something about her odd family, even though she had promised herself never to let Alex know about that side of her. She felt completely naked. Revealed. Would he think she was weird? Would he judge her? Would he think she had a mental illness like his friends had told her?

"That's right; your little brother is at the same school as mine. Victor, right?" Alex asked.

Maya nodded, relieved and a little surprised. "Your brother goes to Fishy Pines as well?"

He nodded. "Yes. I think actually our brothers have become friends lately. Daniel. He went to your house earlier today."

"Wow. I didn't know Daniel was your brother. It really is a small island," Maya said.

"I know," Alex said with a chuckle. "Yet it is strange that the two of us have never hung out together."

"Well, you were one of the popular kids and I... well, I wasn't," Maya said, looking away.

Alex walked closer, grabbed her chin, and lifted her face. He looked into her eyes and moved a lock of hair from her forehead. She could feel his warmth with him so close to her.

"I'm glad we're hanging out now," he said. "I enjoy being with you. I really like you, Maya. I..."

Her heart started to pound hard. Everything about this situation was so strange, so wrong, and yet so right. Her nostrils were filled with the smell of urine. She couldn't believe Alex would even want to be close to her in this instant. At the same time, this was both the worst and the best moment of her life.

"I... like—"

She never got to finish her sentence before Alex placed his lips on hers. Finally—surrounded by the harsh stench of urine—they shared their first real kiss. It wasn't exactly how Maya had pictured it would happen, but it still felt good. No, more than that, it felt amazing.

Maya didn't even notice that, behind her, the shower head had already started dripping.

FIFTY-THREE

"I knew you should never have taken that girl in and hidden her here. Look what that brought you."

Morten was pacing in my kitchen. I had poured myself another glass of wine and sat with it between my hands, still trying to breathe properly. My throat was hurting like crazy and, to be honest, I was still terrified. My legs were shaking.

"Why do you keep doing this to yourself?"

I exhaled. "Not now, Morten. I—"

"You've got to get her out of here. Before she gets you in serious trouble. It might already be too late. That girl belongs somewhere, and you have no right to keep her. I've told you this over and over again. You can't just keep a child."

"Hey. I was helping her, okay? Those guys weren't from some orphanage or social services. They were bad news. You saw them. You really think they wanted what's best for Skye? Because I hardly think so."

He groaned. He was annoying me so much right now. I wasn't exactly in the mood to play the blame game here. I needed time and peace to think. I needed to figure out what to do next.

"She doesn't belong to you. She's not yours to save," Morten said. "Not if it means you'll get hurt in the process. You can't save the entire world, Emma. You just can't. If my job has taught me anything, it's that."

I shook my head. "I can't believe you. Since when did you become so cynical? Of course I can help a girl if she needs me. This is how we change the world, Morten. One person at a time. Showing kindness to those who are put in our lives. Skye came to me for whatever reason, and I take her life very seriously. Right now, I am the only one to protect her from whatever she ran away from. She's my responsibility."

"No, she's not, Emma. She's dangerous. Don't you understand? I'm just concerned about your safety."

I looked at my boyfriend and realized he would never understand. He hadn't seen the look on Daniel's face when he spoke about the place with the cords.

The place where no one hears you scream.

I sipped my wine and shook my head. "I have to protect her."

"I'm not suggesting giving her to those goons out there, Emma. That's not what I'm saying. Call social services. A social worker will find her another home in case she doesn't have one. It's the right thing to do."

I bit my lip. I understood what he was trying to say and, believe me, I had thought about it a thousand times, but something inside of me told me that social services didn't exactly know how to deal with a girl like Skye. She had obviously never been among ordinary people because she had no idea that people had never seen anyone like her. She didn't even try to hide her strange abilities. If she had been a part of the world, she would know to hide them. That's what worried me. She didn't even speak. How would she get by? How would the world receive her?

I knew how the world looked at Victor, and he was even

used to it and knew how to navigate it better, but still, he'd never found his place there. They had no idea how to deal with him. What would they do to a girl like Skye?

I gave Morten a smile, knowing he would never understand.

"I'll look into it after the weekend," I said, mostly to calm him down. All I wanted right now was just some peace and quiet.

Morten sat down with a satisfied sigh and grabbed my hand in his. We sat like that and enjoyed each other's company and the peace and quiet.

It lasted about fifteen minutes.

FIFTY-FOUR

Maria's body jolted upright in bed. Her mind seemed to race around in circles. Something was off, but what?

She had been dreaming about Hanne. They were back at the lab during some of their trials when the glass had broken, and their test subject had attacked Hanne. Maria had been standing there, paralyzed, and not done anything while Hanne was killed, choked to death. She didn't understand why she couldn't react, why she couldn't move, why she didn't help her poor coworker against this threat, and as Hanne slowly died, Maria wondered if it was because she knew she deserved what she got. She knew they all deserved to die for what they had done. No matter how they argued that it was for the betterment of humanity, they had still done the inexcusable. They had been careless, and it was unforgivable.

Hanne had stared at her till the end. Her pleading eyes hadn't left Maria's. Meanwhile, Maria had watched the life of her coworker slowly ooze out of her. Hanne's eyes had pleaded for her help. She had even reached out her hand toward Maria like she expected her to take it, why? Because she was her accomplice. Because they had been in this together. But Maria hadn't offered her a hand. She hadn't helped her.

Next, Maria had found herself inside water, being pulled down and down into it, seeing the light disappear in the distance, trying to swim for the surface, but not moving at all. She remembered feeling how her lungs were filled with water, how she gurgled and couldn't breathe and that was when she woke up, gasping for air. The sensation of suffocation was overwhelming, and even though she knew it had just been a dream, she was still coughing, holding a hand to her throat, trying to get rid of the feeling that still lingered heavily in her body.

Now, she was sitting upright in her bed, listening to the sounds of the night, wondering what was going on. Something wasn't right. It wasn't just the dream. Something was different.

She calmed her breathing and her galloping heart to listen better. There was a sound, a buzzing or almost a humming sound in the house. One that most certainly wasn't supposed to be there.

Maria shot her eyes wide open when realizing what it was. What it could only be.

Water! Someone has turned on the water!

Maria gasped again, then pulled off the covers and jumped out of her bed. She listened a second time just to be sure, but there was no doubt in her mind. That was the sound of water running and the pipes groaning in the old house. Someone had turned on the water. Someone was in the shower.

Alex, she thought. It had to be Alex. But why? Why would he shower at midnight?

Maria realized it didn't really matter and headed into the hallway. She ran toward the bathroom door when she heard a loud scream coming from behind it.

A scream that most certainly didn't come from her oldest son.

FIFTY-FIVE

The water felt wonderful on Maya's face. Alex had left the bathroom to let her wash off the urine stench, and now she was in the shower, letting the water caress her body. She felt tears press in her eyes once again when thinking about this night and how those girls had treated her and how Alex's friends had talked about her. She knew she wasn't exactly popular, but she had never expected them to act that way.

Was it simply because she was dating Alex? He seemed to think so. Because they felt she was a threat from the outside, he had told her. Maya knew the girls were just jealous; there was no doubt there. Alex was a popular guy, one every girl in the school dreamt of dating, but the guys? Why would they be so mean? What did they get out of it? Was it just for the fun of it? Just because they could?

Maya shook the thought. She couldn't let them get to her. This was exactly what they wanted. To make her cry, to make her lose it and maybe decide to never see Alex again. But she wasn't going to do that. She liked him, and he liked her.

"I'm not going to let them get between us. I will not let

them," she said while closing her eyes and letting the water wash the stench and feeling of utter disgust off her.

She decided to think about something nice and pleasant instead, and soon she could only think about the kiss they had shared a few minutes before she stepped into the shower. It had been so soft and sweet and so very gentle. Nothing like when she had kissed Samuel. No, Alex was different.

He was actually a lot different from what she had thought he would be. And when she thought about it, they had a lot more in common than she had believed initially. Both their brothers went to Fishy Pines. Both their mothers were a little off, and they both liked anime. Thinking of it, she had more in common with him than she did with Christina, who was her best friend.

I actually told him about Victor, and he didn't even look at me strangely. He didn't judge me.

It had filled her with such a great sense of relief and, while thinking about it again, she began to chuckle.

She grabbed some shampoo that Alex had told her she could use and washed her hair, rubbing it in thoroughly, making sure to get all the stench off her. The urine had mostly hit her dress, but she felt like it was all over her body and in her hair too. She felt so dirty.

She turned to wash out all the shampoo when a noise made her open her eyes. It sounded like it came from beneath her and she looked down at the drain with a light gasp. It sounded almost like the drain was groaning, and the groaning soon turned to a loud humming that soon became like a banging.

"Probably just the old pipes," Maya told herself. She said it loudly because it made her feel calmer.

She knew this entire island had very old pipes underneath it and she had often heard that they groaned, especially in the older houses. She had heard it in her own house too, but never this loud. Maya stood for a few seconds and listened. It was almost like the banging was rhythmical. Like there was a rhythm to it. Like it was playing a melody.

CLINK-CLANK-CLINK. CLINK-CLANK-CLINK.

And then it stopped.

Maya stared at the drain below her, then shrugged. She returned to her showering and closed her eyes to wash off the rest of the shampoo when she heard another sound, the distinct sound of something slithering and gliding, and then she felt something touch her foot, something wet and slimy.

Maya opened her eyes with a loud gasp and looked down. A set of very blue eyes stared back up at her from the drain. Clawed hands shaped from clear water reached up toward her.

As they grabbed her, Maya finally screamed.

FIFTY-SIX

Oh, dear Lord, someone is in trouble!

Hearing the screams, Maria rushed for the bathroom door, then opened it, slamming it up against the wall. Inside, she saw exactly what she had feared to see one day.

Maria couldn't breathe. The girl—whom she had no idea who it was—screamed and cried for help as the water creature used her legs to pull itself out of the drain, slithering up her body, then began gushing water into her, forcing it into her. She gurgled and spurted, tried to block the water or move away from it, but clearly could not breathe properly.

"Oh, my God, Maya."

The voice was Alexander's. He came up behind Maria and was about to jump to the girl's aid when Maria grabbed him and pulled him back forcefully.

"Don't, Alex."

He stared at his mother, confusion in his terror-filled eyes. "What are you talking about, Mom? I have to help Maya. She's in trouble," Alex yelled.

"You'll be killed," Maria said, her heart pounding in her chest as she remembered Hanne lying on the floor of the restroom. Maria stood firm, holding her son back, and while Maya fought for her life, Maria remained paralyzed just like she had been in that awful dream.

"Mom, let go of me. I need to help her!"

Alex yelled and screamed at her, then finally managed to tear himself loose and ran toward the girl in the shower. As he did, the water creature gave up on the girl, turned its blobby head, looked at Alex, then like a wave, threw itself at Maria's son, overwhelming him and forcing him to the tiles, pressing him down underneath the massive wave of gushing water.

"NO!"

Exhausted, Maya fell to the bathroom floor, coughing and throwing up water, gasping and gurgling. Meanwhile, Maria stared at her poor son, but the creature wasn't very interested in him, she could tell. And she knew why.

It hadn't come for the girl or for Alex. It had come for her. Maria had been hiding for so long. It was time to face her fate.

"I'm here," she said, stepping forward into the light, knowing that the creature couldn't see very well in brightly lit surroundings. Its eyes were better at night or in complete darkness where it could navigate through the drains and pipes.

"I'm the one you've come for. I'm the one you want, right? So, take me. Take me instead."

At the sound of her voice, the creature let go of Alexander immediately and focused on Maria instead. Turning itself into a wave, it rushed toward her, flushing water at her so fast she was knocked to the floor. Through the pouring water, she spotted Daniel, her youngest son, staring back at her.

His eyes were the last thing she ever saw.

FIFTY-SEVEN

I had just finished my wine when I received the call. Morten and I were sitting in silence till the sound of my vibrating phone cut through it.

It was Maya. She was crying heavily, and it was hard for me to understand what she was saying.

"Mom. Please come. Something happened. Something terrible," was what I got out of her and that she was at Alex's house. It was all I needed.

"What's going on?" Morten asked when I hung up. I rushed to the hallway and grabbed my coat, then put on my boots, not caring that I put them on the wrong feet, while yelling at him.

"Maya is in trouble. Stay here with Victor and Skye."

Before he could object, I was out of the house, running to my car. I had no idea what I was going to face, but I could tell Maya was terrified, and that was enough for me. I fumbled with the keys, jumped inside the car, and rushed off, driving through the snow, my heart throbbing in my chest.

What was she doing at Alex's house? What could have scared her so much? Was it Alex? Had he hurt her somehow?

Luckily, they lived so close that it took me less than a

minute to get there. I didn't even turn off the car. I simply hit the brakes, then jumped out, leaving the keys in it.

"Oh, God, please let her be all right. Please, let her be fine."

She called me. That means she's good, right?

"Maya," I called as I knocked on the door and pressed the doorbell again and again. It took a few seconds before it opened. I can't remember ever being happier to see my daughter's face, even though she was wearing nothing but a towel. I attacked her in a huge embrace.

"Maya. Oh, you scared me. Are you okay?"

She was soaking wet. I touched her hair while she hugged me.

"It was awful, Mom... I..."

"Have you been in the shower? What are you doing here? Maya? I don't understand anything right now; please explain." Maya looked into my eyes. Then she started to cry. "She's dead."

"Who's dead?" I asked, startled.

"Alex's mother. There was something in the drain... I... I was taking a shower, and something came up and grabbed me, and then his mom came in and... and then Alex was there and he... then he was attacked and then his mom... she... she..."

Maya could hardly speak anymore. Tears were streaming across her cheeks, and her words were hard to understand because she was speaking between gasps.

"Who killed her, Maya?" I asked, worried it was Alex and that Maya once again had fallen in love with a killer.

"A thing... I don't know what it was. It was water, and then it was not... then it had eyes and hands... hands with claws, and it reached up toward me and grabbed me... and it had a face, Mommy; oh, it was so gross, so nasty."

Maya shuddered and hugged me tighter. I held her for a few seconds more. There were so many things I didn't understand right now, like why my daughter was naked, showering at her boyfriend's house, but I decided now was not the time.

"Where are Alex and Daniel?" I asked.

"Upstairs."

"And where is the animal or creature or whatever you'd call it?"

"Disappeared into the drain after it killed her. I am never taking a shower again, Mom. Never."

FIFTY-EIGHT

"You said there was another boy. She had another son."

Morten's colleague, Allan, looked up from his pad. I had called the police station after finding the body of Maria Finnerup in the bathroom. I was now sitting in her living room with Maya leaning her head on my shoulder and Alexander seated in a chair across from us, hiding his face between his hands.

"Yes," I said. "Daniel is his name. He's her youngest. He was here earlier, right, Maya?"

Maya nodded. She was still shaking and clinging to me. "I'm pretty sure I saw him here when... when his mother... he was standing in the hallway, and he saw her. It all went so fast, though. I'm not sure what I saw anymore."

"But he's not here now," I said. "He wasn't here when I got here either. He might have run away when he saw what happened to his mother."

"We'll look for him," Allan said, then sighed and tapped his pen on the pad where he had written down everything we had told him.

"And you say that the water spurted up from the drain and simply drowned her?" he continued.

"Yes," I said. "It flooded everything. Must have been a cracked pipe or something. The kids were lucky they survived."

It wasn't a lie, but it wasn't the truth either. I had told both kids that there was no way the police would believe them if they began to talk about a liquefied creature seeping up through the drains to attack them. They would end up like Laila Lund. The world wasn't ready to know the truth.

"I've called their dad in California, and he's gonna try to get back as fast as possible," he said.

"The kids can stay with me till he gets here," I said.

"All right," Allan said. "Guess we'll go search for Daniel as soon as Dr. Williamsen finishes. But you're free to go. Do you want me to take you home or can you drive?"

"I'm fine," I said and got up.

Maya was still holding on to me like she was afraid I might leave her. I kissed the top of her head, and we walked over to Alex. I reached out my hand and put it on his shoulder.

"Come on, Alex. We're leaving now."

He didn't look up. He rose to his feet and simply followed us outside. I put my arm around his shoulder and guided him to the car. Maya got in the back with him, and they held on to each other while I drove back to my house.

Morten was waiting in the kitchen. He got up when we came inside. I had called ahead and told him what had happened. I had told him there was a leak and that Alex's mother had been killed by the water. I didn't enjoy lying to him, but Morten simply wouldn't understand. And I didn't want to discuss it with him. I was afraid he would just claim that Alex and Maya were drunk. They had, after all, been to a party.

"You want something to drink?" Morten asked me after Maya had helped Alex up the stairs. I had told her he could sleep in the room next to hers, but I had a feeling they were going to hang out in her room for a little while. Alex had to be very worried about his younger brother, and I didn't think he'd be able to sleep till he was found, if he would sleep at all tonight, the poor kid. He seemed in such a deep state of shock I wasn't sure he even realized what had happened.

"I could do with a whiskey right now," I said.

"That bad, huh?" he asked and found two glasses. He went to the cabinet in the living room then came back with an old bottle and poured us each a whiskey. He handed me one.

"It was supposed to be such a great night for us," I said. "I'm sorry."

"Well, if there is one thing I've learned over the years, it's that life with you is never boring or even predictable, Emma."

"I'll drink to that," I said, and we clinked glasses.

FIFTY-NINE

The drink knocked me out completely. Just like I had hoped it would. I fell asleep on the couch, and I guess Morten must have decided just to leave me there and go sleep in my bed because, when I woke up, I had a blanket on top of me, and I was all alone.

It took me a few seconds to remember what had happened, but once I did, a tear escaped my eye while thinking about the two boys who now had to go on without their dear mother. How would Daniel react? If he was anything like Victor, his world would completely crumble. For kids like him, it was vital that everything remain the way it always was. Changes could throw them completely off balance. And this certainly was a huge change.

I felt so terribly worried about the poor boy.

I sat up on the couch, looking out into the garden where the moon shone on the ocean behind the trees. The glistening snow reflected the moonshine and lit up the entire area. It looked beautiful, so incredibly peaceful.

It was while sitting there, looking outside, that I realized what had woken me up. It wasn't a dream or because I was worried. It was something else. There was a sound. The sound of dripping. I used to think it was a tap that wasn't closed properly, or maybe a leak, but I knew better by now. I remembered hearing the sound a few times before, and it scared me.

Whatever this creature was, was it coming for me next?

I took a few deep breaths, then walked to the fireplace and grabbed a poker. With cautious steps, I walked to the downstairs bathroom and stood outside the door for a few seconds, wondering what to do next.

Then I opened the door.

I stared for a few seconds at what my eyes saw in there, not quite grasping what I was looking at.

"D-Daniel?"

I dropped the poker and rushed to him. He was sitting on the bathroom floor on his knees, looking at his hand.

"Oh, dear God, I am glad to see you," I said and sat next to him. "We've been looking everywhere for you. The police are probably still out there searching the entire island to find you, and you were here all the time."

The boy looked up at me, and that was when I realized why he was looking at his hand so intently.

"D-Daniel? What's wrong with your hand? What's happening to it?" I asked, startled.

His very clear blue eyes met mine. "I... I don't know."

It was like his hand had melted. Like it had... liquefied itself. And now it was... dripping onto my tiles.

What the heck?

"Daniel... A-are you... I mean, can you?" I stopped myself. I had no idea how to ask what I was about to ask. Fact was, I wondered if he was the creature, if he somehow was the one who had killed all those people, but somehow it didn't really fit. Why would he do that? He was nothing but a sweet young boy. Why would he kill his own mother?

He sniffled. "It happens sometimes," he said. "And not just

to my hand. Also to my feet. One day it was my earlobe. It simply started to drip onto my shoulder."

"So, you can't control it."

Maybe that was the answer. That he couldn't control himself when it happened. Could that be it? Maybe he didn't know what he did.

Oh, God, did the boy kill his own mother without knowing it?

I reached out for the poker and pulled it closer while staring at Daniel's hand. If he was about to turn liquid, turn into whatever this creature was, would I even stand a chance? Would my family?

It was while wondering about this that I heard the pipes groaning in the walls. The groans soon turned to banging, and I turned to look at the shower, particularly at the drain.

SIXTY

I stared at the drain, paralyzed, my heart throbbing in my throat so hard I could hardly bear it. The pipes groaned and moaned, and something emerged from inside the drain, slithering its way through the small holes, emerging into my bathroom.

As the creature grew out of the water and rose up in front of me, I backed up, poker in my hand, protecting Daniel behind me.

A set of very blue eyes looked back at me from inside the water. It approached me, slithering its way quickly across the bathroom floor, and when it was close enough, I swung the poker with a loud cry.

"Stay away from the boy!"

Of course, the thing went straight through it. It was just like hitting water. The creature didn't even react, it just continued toward me, gushing at me, and soon I was completely soaked by a wave so hard it knocked me down. Water gushed into my eyes, my mouth and down my throat with such speed that I couldn't even react or move.

I wanted to yell at Daniel to run, to get out of there while he could, but it was impossible. Water was everywhere, and all I could see were the creature's eyes staring at me from somewhere inside of it, such deep anger and hatred in them. I didn't even see Daniel rise to his feet. But somewhere from outside of the thick pillar of water, I heard him yell a muffled cry.

"STOP!"

Much to my surprise, the creature did as he said. The water stopped gushing and was sucked back to where it had originated, shaping the creature into what more and more looked like... a woman.

I coughed and threw up water, then looked up. The woman seemed to solidify herself and soon looked completely human.

"Mommy!" Daniel exclaimed. "You can't kill her. She didn't do anything. She's been good to me."

Mommy?

"Danny," the woman said, her voice still sounding like she was in water, but as she spoke more, the voice turned normal. "Are you okay?"

He nodded. The woman held out her arms, and the boy rushed into her embrace. They hugged while I got back to my feet, still coughing and still fighting the feeling of suffocation.

I sat on the top of the toilet and looked at the two of them. "So... if she's your mother, then who was Maria?"

The woman looked at me. "She took him from me."

"Maria did? Why?"

"Because of who he is and what he can do."

I sighed. "I don't understand. Could you please explain?"

The woman looked at her son briefly, then kissed him.

"It's okay, Mommy," Daniel said. "She's the good one. Remember, she took care of B-3? And she has been taking care of Victor."

"B-3, that's Skye, right? We call her Skye," I said. "You know her too?"

The woman nodded. "She escaped with me."

"Escaped?" I paused. "Let me guess. Omicon? That's the

place with the cords, right? The place where no one can hear you scream?"

Daniel nodded. "I was born there."

"Maybe we should tell her the story from the beginning, huh?" the woman said.

I exhaled in relief. "Thank you. I'd appreciate that."

SIXTY-ONE

"I came here in nineteen eighty-two. Through the sewers, through the island's pipes," the woman who told me her name was Lyn—which meant waterfall—said. "I was found and pulled out of a toilet by a man. I was just a child back then."

"Through the sewers?" I asked, thinking about Samuel, who had told us a similar story.

She nodded.

"Where did you come from?"

"A place very different from this. A place of war. My parents sent me through the tunnels to escape, to get to safety. It was believed that the tunnels led to a different world, one where we could live in peace, but most people thought it was just superstition. My parents believed. They wanted a better life for me. A lot of parents did the same.

"We entered the tunnels and came here. Our parents would come later, they said. But they never did. Some drowned in the water, but many of us managed to survive. Some of us didn't end up in a better place. Instead, we were taken by men in black clothes and experimented on. I was pulled out of a toilet by a plumber and a nurse. Three others and I were there. But when the nurse called for help, those men came, and they killed the plumber.

"The entire building containing the restroom where we had come through was closed off. They kept us there for years before they transported us somewhere else. To a building with no windows. I was placed in a room with no escape. The men and women did terrible things to us there."

"Sven Thomsen," I said. "Ann Mortensen, Hanne Carlsen, Maria Finnerup. They all worked there, didn't they?"

"They made me with child. Using human semen. Wanted to create a superhuman, they said. For war. Soon, I gave birth to twins. A girl and a boy." Lyn's face darkened. She looked down at her son.

"But as soon as the babies were born, they were taken from me. I could hear them scream for me at night. They did things to them. Unimaginable things. They wanted to see if the children were like me, but they weren't. But they kept pushing, kept putting them into water, holding them down, trying to force them to change, to be like me.

"One day, when the twins were eight, they told me my daughter... she didn't survive. They had killed her. Drowned her. They went too far, thinking if she stayed long enough underwater, she would change. But she didn't. She died. Drowned in that tank of theirs. I spent years in grief and anger, planning how to get back at them for what they had done.

"Recently, I managed to escape through the sewers one night when they were so careless that they forgot to plug the keyhole to the room they kept me in. I squeezed through it, then rushed for the restroom. I swore I would stop them, stop what they were doing. I managed to take B-3 with me because she was in the room next to me, and when she saw me rush out, she spoke to me in my mind, pleaded with me to take her too, but I lost her somehow once we got out.

"I had actually thought she died in the water because it was a very long swim for her. I went looking for Daniel, who was living with another family now, while they waited for his change to come. I've been keeping an eye on him, and on B-3, after I realized where she was, that she was here. I only did to those people what they did to my daughter. And now, all I want is to be with my son."

Lyn kissed his forehead, and Daniel closed his eyes. Then something happened as the two of them hugged. It was like they both turned to liquid and their two bodies became one. It lasted only for a few seconds, till they both returned to normal.

Lyn realized what had happened, then exhaled with a smile.

"Look, Mommy," Daniel said. "I am like you. Well... almost."

Lyn sighed and held her son close, a concerned look in her eyes.

"They will come for him," she said. "He can't survive in the water yet. It's still too new, and he might have too much human in him. We don't know yet."

She turned her head and looked at me. "Can he stay here? I'm looking for a way back to where we came from. When I find it, I'll come for him. But for now, I need a safe place for him to be. You have kept B-3 safe. You can do the same for my son."

My eyes grew wide. "I... I don't know."

Lyn grabbed my arm and squeezed it, her pleading eyes lingering on me. "Please. I have nowhere else to turn. I can't send him back to those people. The father in that family, he's part of it too. If they find out what he can do, what they have created, there is no telling what they'll do to him."

"I have his older brother, Alex, sleeping upstairs," I said.

"Don't let him see Daniel. Don't tell the father or anyone else. Keep him hidden till I come back. I am certain I will find the way back soon. If there is a way into this world, there must be a way out."

I swallowed, feeling slight anxiety growing, thinking about the men I had faced earlier in the night. But how could I say no to a mother who wanted to keep her son safe?

"All right," I said. "But the killings must stop. They might deserve it, but it solves nothing, Lyn."

"Deal."

Lyn reached out her hand, and I grabbed it. It felt like a human hand at first but then turned wobbly as she slowly turned to liquid and soon was nothing but a puddle. The puddle then moved toward the drain where it disappeared down the holes.

"Mommy!" Daniel said and rushed toward the shower.

"She'll be back, Daniel," I said and put my arm around his shoulder. "You heard her. She'll be back for you."

SIXTY-TWO

She let Alex sleep in her room. She knew he wasn't supposed to, but he had been so out of it, she thought it was for the best. Finally, he had fallen asleep after crying in her arms for hours, but Maya was still wide awake. She couldn't let go of all the emotions, all the thoughts rushing through her mind.

What the heck had she seen tonight? What was that thing that had almost killed her and ended up killing Alex's mother? Calling it a creature or a monster somehow didn't quite suffice. This thing was a lot more than that. She had felt it when it had tried to kill her.

Maya shivered again, even though she was under the covers in her bed. Alex was sleeping on an air mattress next to her, snoring lightly, twisting in his sleep, sometimes moaning.

Maya had to pee. She had felt the desire for at least two hours but completely ignored it. She didn't dare to go to the bathroom. Not after what she had faced tonight. Not in the darkness at night. She wanted to wait till the morning before going and tried to ignore it, but the sensation grew more and more insistent, especially when she tried to not think about it, and it was keeping her awake.

Think of something else. Think of a meadow. A meadow, a meadow, a meadow.

She pictured it and closed her eyes. There were yellow flowers, there was corn, maybe even a bird, and over there... was a small brook, the water running quickly through it. Soon, the sound of running water was trickling inside her head, and her eyes shot open once again, the desire to go to the bathroom screaming inside her.

Think of Alex kissing you.

She did and closed her eyes again. Alex's lips, Alex's soft eyes, Alex's warmth close to her... in the bathroom, where water was running.

Maya opened her eyes again with a groan. It was no use. She'd have to go to the bathroom even though it scared her senseless. She got up out of bed, then rushed to the door and into the bathroom where she relieved herself faster than ever before, constantly staring at the shower drain next to her, whimpering because she felt it took too long to go. Finally, when she was done, she washed her hands quickly and rushed into the hallway, where she ran into her mother. Someone was with her.

"Daniel?" she asked, then smiled. "They found him?"

Her mother nodded. "Well... he came to us. Let's just keep it at that."

"Great, Alex will be very excited to hear this."

Her mother exhaled. "Well... about that. He can't know, I'm afraid."

"What? Why not?"

"It's a long story, honey. I'd love to tell you everything, but can it wait? I need to sleep. Maybe we can talk about it in the morning."

"Mom... I can't just keep this news from Alex. How am I supposed to do that?"

"You have to," her mother said. "There are bad people after

Daniel. Just trust me on this, will you? It's also what's best for Alex. The less he knows, the better."

Maya sighed, annoyed. She could hear an urgency and sincerity in her mother's voice, and she knew this was important. "Okay. But I need an explanation and soon."

"And I will give it to you. Just... well, just do as I told you... for now. Not even Morten can know he's here, okay?"

Maya shot her mother a glance. "Okay... I guess."

SIXTY-THREE

I found a clean sheet and put it on the bed in one of my empty rooms. I was beginning to count myself lucky for having inherited this big old house with so many bedrooms. When I first moved in, I thought I would never have a use for all these bedrooms. But I guess life had different plans.

Daniel sat on the bed. I found a blanket and a pillow for him and sat down next to him.

"Are you okay?"

He nodded.

I looked down at his hand. It remained completely human. I still couldn't quite grasp what I had seen earlier, how both he and his mother had changed their bodies. How was it even physically possible? It defied everything I knew. I wasn't surprised that the scientists had kept this a secret or that they wanted to exploit their abilities. In the wrong hands, a soldier who could turn himself into liquid and slip in anywhere could become very dangerous. But the boy who sat next to me was no soldier. It was just a young boy, a scared young boy who had no idea what was happening to him or how to control it.

"Can I ask you something, Daniel?"

He looked up at me. "Sure."

"What color is your blood?"

He looked down at his hand briefly, then back at me. "Green."

I nodded with an exhale. "I thought so." I put the pillow in place. "Now, I suggest we get some sleep. It's been quite a day. I, for one, can't wait to get some shut-eye."

Daniel laid himself down. "I'm scared," he whispered. "Of the dark."

I sighed. I couldn't say I was surprised. With all he had been through, I'd bet it wasn't just the dark that scared him.

I sang a song for him, one of those that Victor used to want me to sing before bedtime. Before Skye came along. Daniel's eyes were big and wide, staring up at me. After I had stopped singing, I stood in the doorway while Daniel got comfortable. I waited a few seconds till his breathing got heavy before I turned the lights off. I couldn't stop wondering about Victor.

The green blood. The abilities that seemed out of this world. Victor shared those things. Did that mean he was one of them too? But how was that even possible? I had given birth to him. He didn't come from some other world. I knew he didn't.

"I don't think he even is your son."

That was what Samuel had told me. He had wanted my son because of his blood. I had never felt like Victor belonged here in this world and I still didn't. But he was my son. Wasn't he?

I never finished the thought—awful as it was—but closed the door to Daniel's bedroom and wandered into my bedroom, where Morten was snoring loudly. I got under the covers and closed my eyes, but sleep didn't come at first. Instead, I lay awake for a few minutes, wondering how I was supposed to fall asleep with that noise. Yet a few minutes later, I did.

SIXTY-FOUR

I was awakened by heavy steps outside in the hallway, and then my door was slammed open. I sat up with a small gasp, shocked and annoyed to be ripped out of my pleasant dream of our holiday to Greece. Instead of the azure blue ocean and the bright summer light, I was staring at my son, who, for once, was looking directly at me.

"Victor?" I asked.

"Where is she?" he asked, almost hissed.

I blinked. "Where's who?"

"Skye!"

"I don't know, sweetie," I said. "Is she not in your room?"

"She was gone when I woke up."

"Well, I don't know, Victor. I've been sleeping. Don't you think she's downstairs or maybe in the garden? Maybe she woke up early and went outside. You know how she loves it out there."

"She's not there," he said, angrily. "Where is she?"

"I told you I don't know," I said as the night's many activities came back to me and I remembered Daniel and his mother and all that had happened with them.

Morten was waking up now, rubbing his eyes. "What time is it?"

I looked at the clock. "It's seven," I said, annoyed. "It's Saturday, Victor. Couldn't you have let us sleep in a little?"

"She's not here!" he said, alarmed.

I got out of bed and hurried to his room, suddenly feeling anxious. I opened the door and found it empty.

"She's not here," I said.

"That's what I said," Victor complained. "Stop stating the obvious."

"And you checked downstairs?" I said and rushed to the bathroom, but it was empty too. Then I walked down the stairs and called her name.

"Skye? Skye?"

But there was no answer. I walked to the back door and looked out the window. I even looked up in the trees. Nothing. Yet there was something, and it made my blood freeze over. Out in the snow in the garden and on the porch steps leading to the house were what looked like hundreds of footprints. I opened the door and looked at them, my heart pounding. Those were no ordinary footprints. These were heavy boots in a size none of us wore in the house. It had been snowing most of the night, so they had to be very fresh. I stood by them, then looked up at Victor's window above.

Could they have...?

Morten came out after me. "What are you doing out here in the cold?"

"They took her," I said. Tears were pressing behind my eyes, and I tried to hold them back. Victor was standing in the doorway, his small body beginning to shake.

"Who took whom?" Morten asked, rubbing his forehead. "I'm not quite following you here."

"The men. Those men from last night. They were in my house while we slept. They took her, Morten. They took her."

Morten stared at me, then shook his head. "Nonsense. That's impossible. We would have heard it."

"She's gone, Morten. Skye's gone."

He threw out his hands. "Well, maybe she ran away again. She didn't really belong here; maybe she went back home, huh? How about we go inside? It's too cold out here."

I shook my head. "Didn't you hear me? Those men took Skye!"

"You're being paranoid," Morten said and pulled me back inside.

"Maybe she just took a walk. She might be back in a few hours. Let's not jump to any conclusions here."

"Why won't you listen, Morten?" I said and pulled my arm out of his grip. "They took her."

"How did they get in, huh?"

"I don't know. They have their ways, I guess."

"Okay and what about the dogs, huh? Brutus would have eaten them alive if they came inside the bedroom."

I looked at Victor. "Brutus."

Victor ran ahead of me as we rushed upstairs, Morten still yelling at us that we were acting paranoid and to calm down.

But there was no Brutus inside his room. Kenneth slept with Maya, and he would never have reacted. To anything else, yes, but never to dangerous situations.

"Brutus?"

"Brutus?" Victor called, his small voice shivering.

"Maybe she took him for a walk," Morten said, finally catching up to us.

I gave him a look when we heard a scrape coming from inside Victor's wardrobe, and he ran to open it.

"Brutus!" I said and rushed to the dog. He was lying on his side and still half asleep. I looked at Morten.

"Now, don't you see?"

"See what? The dog is sleeping."

"First, this dog never sleeps. Second, how did he get in the wardrobe, huh?" I asked.

Morten nodded. "Okay, that is strange; I'll give you that. But who knows with this dog? He's always been a little... peculiar."

I helped Victor get Brutus out of the wardrobe. He tried to lift his head and look at Victor, but it fell back down.

"They must have sedated him somehow," I said. "It'll wear off. Don't worry, Victor. He'll be fine."

Victor caressed the dog while letting a couple of tears roll down his cheeks. I let him tend to the dog while panic erupted inside me. I knew these people had to work for Omicon, and they had probably taken Skye back to that awful lab.

The place where no one hears you scream.

How was I supposed to get her out of there again?

I had barely finished the thought when Morten's phone rang. He rushed into the bedroom and picked it up, then came back a few seconds later, completely pale.

"What's wrong?"

"It's... it's Jytte. She's in the hospital. A fishing boat pulled her out of the ocean this morning. She's at the hospital in Esbjerg on the mainland."

"Oh, dear God, Morten, what... how?"

He swallowed. His eyes were in complete shock. "I... I have to go."

"Let me take you," I said. "You're in no condition to be driving. Maya is home; she can look after Victor."

"Allan is picking me up. He's the one who called. I'll... I'll call you later."

SIXTY-FIVE

I paced in the kitchen for hours, waiting for news from Morten, but none came. I was so worried about Jytte and about him, it drove me nuts. Victor was inconsolable. Even after Alex was picked up by his father and taken home and I showed Victor that Daniel was here with us, it didn't seem to cheer him up at all.

He sulked all day, sitting in the corner of the kitchen, looking at the floor. It just about broke my heart. Brutus woke up and came down to be with him. It was sweet how that big ugly dog could sense he needed him. And he did. Victor needed him more than ever.

I made breakfast for all the kids, including Maya, whom I had a long chat with as soon as Alex had been picked up and they had hugged goodbye. I told her the entire story from the night before, about Daniel and his mother and even though I could tell it was a little much for my young girl, she seemed to understand what I was telling her by the time I told her that Lyn had asked me to take care of the boy and not tell anyone.

"I just don't know how to... I mean, I think we're dating now. I don't quite know if he'll still want to after all this, you know losing his mother and all," she said. "But I don't want to lie to him."

"I'm afraid you'll have to," I said. "At least for a while. I don't like lying to Morten, but I have had to do it a lot lately."

"Maybe Alex would understand if I told him the entire story," she said.

I shook my head violently. "No, Maya. We can't run that risk. These people took Skye last night. They're dangerous. If Morten hadn't been there last night, there's no telling what they might have done to me. They tried to hurt me, Maya. You would also be putting Alex in danger if he knew and had to keep it a secret. Please, Maya. It's best this way."

She sighed. "All right. Hopefully, it won't be long."

Sophia stopped by later and took a quick glance at Daniel. "If you keep this up, you're gonna have more children than I do."

I poured us both some coffee and we sat down. Then I began to cry. I told her the entire story about Daniel, his mother, and Skye, who had disappeared, and then about Morten, whom I hadn't heard from all day, and I was about to die from worry.

"What if Jytte dies? I mean, they said she was still alive when they brought her in, but what if..."

Sophia stopped me. "You can't do the what ifs."

I sighed and sipped my coffee when there was a knock on my door. I rushed out and opened it.

Outside stood Morten.

I nearly dropped my jaw. "Morten? How? How is she?"

"She's awake," he said.

I exhaled, relieved. "Oh, thank God... what was she doing?"

"She took pills," he interrupted me.

"What?"

He swallowed. He was even paler than this morning. "She took pills, then jumped into the ocean in the middle of the night. Because she was lonely, she said. Because she didn't want to live anymore."

"I... I... that's awful, Morten. Do you want to come inside?" I asked.

He shook his head, and that was when I noticed a shift in his eyes. Something had changed, something deep within him.

"You're blaming me, aren't you?" I asked. "Because I asked you to stay last night." I shook my head while tears piled up in my eyes. "You're thinking she would never have done this if you'd been home, if I... I hadn't asked you to...?"

He didn't dispute it. Instead, he shook his head. "I... I have to get back to the hospital. I only came to get some of her stuff."

"So... so, where does this leave us?" I asked.

His eyes avoided mine. "I need to focus on her right now," he said. "I didn't know it was this bad. I've overlooked a lot of signs. I don't want that to happen again. She needs me, Emma. I need to be with her and take care of her. Full-time."

"So... so, this is it? For us?" I asked, half choking.

He exhaled and took a step away from me. "I can't ask you to wait for me."

"But I will," I said.

"I can't ask you to do that. I don't know how long it will take. I can't promise you it'll ever get better."

"So, what are you saying?" I said with a sniffle. "This is it?"

"I... I guess so," he said. He lifted his head and looked into my eyes.

"But... Morten?"

"I'm sorry, Emma. I really, truly am."

And with those words, he turned around and walked to his car. I felt like screaming and yelling at him, demanding him to stop, yelling that I would wait for him no matter how long it took, but no words left my lips. Instead, I watched him drive away, taking a big chunk of my poor aching heart with him.

When I finally made it back into the kitchen, Sophia had already poured me a whiskey.

"Guess it's back to being just us, huh?"

I downed the entire drink in one gulp and put the glass down. Sophia poured me a second one, and I sat down, my body feeling heavy and so incredibly tired. We sat there, staring into our drinks for a few minutes, no one saying a word. I couldn't stop thinking about Morten and all we had together, and how mad I was at him for ending it like this, for throwing it all away. But also, how I understood him completely. I would have done the same if it had been Maya. We both knew I would.

"So... how are we going to get Skye back from that place, huh?" Sophia asked and downed her drink as well.

I lifted my head and looked at her, then emptied my glass. As I put the glass down, I sucked in air between my teeth.

"I think I might have an idea."

Sophia chuckled.

"That's what I thought. I have never known Emma Frost just to sit there and feel sorry for herself. At least not for very long."

A LETTER FROM WILLOW

Dear Reader,

I want to say a huge thank you for choosing to read *Drip Drop Dead*. If you enjoyed it and want to keep up to date with all my latest releases, just sign up at the following link. Your email address will never be shared, and you can unsubscribe at any time.

www.bookouture.com/willow-rose

I hope you loved *Drip Drop Dead* and if you did, I would be very grateful if you could write a review. I'd love to hear what you think, and it makes such a difference helping new readers to discover one of my books for the first time.

As always, I want to thank you for all your support and for reading my books. I love hearing from my readers—you can get in touch through social media or my website, or email me at madamewillowrose@gmail.com.

Take care,

Willow

KEEP IN TOUCH WITH WILLOW

www.willow-rose.net

facebook.com/willowredrose

x.com/madamwillowrose

instagram.com/willowroseauthor

bookbub.com/authors/willow-rose

PUBLISHING TEAM

Turning a manuscript into a book requires the efforts of many people. The publishing team at Bookouture would like to acknowledge everyone who contributed to this publication.

Commercial
Lauren Morrissette
Hannah Richmond
Imogen Allport

Cover design
The Brewster Project

Data and analysis
Mark Alder
Mohamed Bussuri

Editorial
Jennifer Hunt
Sinead O'Connor

Proofreader
Joni Wilson

Marketing
Alex Crow
Melanie Price
Occy Carr
Cíara Rosney
Martyna Młynarska

Operations and distribution
Marina Valles
Stephanie Straub

Production
Hannah Snetsinger
Mandy Kullar
Jen Shannon

Publicity
Kim Nash
Noelle Holten
Jess Readett
Sarah Hardy

Rights and contracts
Peta Nightingale
Richard King
Saidah Graham

Milton Keynes UK
Ingram Content Group UK Ltd.
UKHW011432140724
445326UK00004B/125